THE GIVEN

INTERLAND SERIES BOOK #1

GARY CLARK

GCL BOOKS

CONTENTS

For Jude

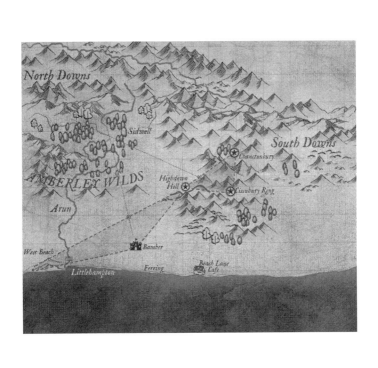

PROLOGUE

L isten. I'll tell you a story. When I was a boy, a young and handsome adventurer, I embarked on a quest through the Amberley Wilds. I was drawn to uncover the myth of the Interland. I was chasing a dream, a vision of a place in legend that had lodged in my mind. It took hold of me and wouldn't let go.

The Wilds are so thick that they're impossible to navigate in any meaningful sense – you have to just feel your way. My grandmother used to say that the only way to get through the Wilds is to connect with the energy of Nature, and then flow with it – push in the same direction, don't resist it.

So I pressed bravely through the thick undergrowth, seeking my connection. Brambles tore my skin and mosquitos raised welts in my neck. Doubt crept in as I grew cold, hungry, and scared. But something pushed me on and sometime before dusk I stumbled into a clearing on the bankside where the river widened onto a flood plain.

I felt a charge in the air. Dusk drew in, and a thin mist hung over the river. The smooth surface of the water stood black and still like a painting. Poppies in the fields waved in the breeze, *scenting the air. A wooden raft, its logs tied with vine, stuck lodged against the bank like an invitation. I climbed aboard.*

After a few minutes drifting through fog, the river narrowed, and I picked up speed. With the wind in my face, the current took me straight to a sheer face of rock, where the river disappeared into a cave.

The gateway to the Interland is where the three rivers of the Wilds meet, converging at a magical pool, an oasis of energy at the heart of the wilderness. The charge was electric as I passed through the hill, a tunnel of rock, and into the pool - the Gateway - where an intricate beehive of caves stretched deep into the earth. I was mesmerised. I felt the energy in the ground, the stone walls, and the Wilds. But more than that, I was a part of it - that delicate interdependence between us and our environment. I was at one with Nature. For the first time in my life, I was free.

PART I

RESISTANCE

1

J ay sat cross-legged on the roof where the sloping tiles connected with the house next door. She gazed across the fields towards the hills of Devil's Dyke. The wind off the sea gave a vicious whip as it rose over the sand and through the Beach Lane housing estate, and Jay sensed frustration in the air. Something was coming. She closed her book, stifling the wind-ruffled pages.

'Jay!' Her dad's voice from downstairs. He called again, his tone more urgent. She climbed through the Velux window to her room. Over her shoulder she glimpsed the flickering light of a fire up on Highdown Hill and she paused for a moment to watch. Her dad called again, and she turned to head downstairs.

Jay avoided the kitchen and made straight for the dining room where her brother Sammy was laying the table. He rolled his eyes at the noise coming through the wall. Jay took four place mats from the cupboard and arranged them on the table. 'What now?'

'Same as always,' said Sammy.

'Anything and everything?'

'Exactly.'

Their mum, Sonia, was *challenged*, to use the words of Jay's best friend, Stitch. She struggled to exist in the world. She was bitter, jealous of everyone. She made Jay feel like she and her brother had done her a terrible injustice just by existing in the world; it was a powerless feeling. Sonia used to drink, not much, but it only took a single glass of wine to bring on her aggression. It wasn't that she threw fists or anything. She would stalk around the house seeking out someone to find fault with. Jay and Sammy learned to stay out of sight, tiptoe, avoid attention.

'Here we are,' Jay's dad, Ben, said as he entered the dining room, placing two bowls of spaghetti bolognese on the table.

Sonia flicked on the television on the sideboard and waved her hand for Ben to shift up so that she could take her favourite seat. Ben shuffled up next to Jay, giving her a wink. Back when she and Sammy were small, when her powers were beginning to surface and life was confusing enough, their parents' arguments scared and confused her. Not so much now. She'd turned 18 last month, and that magic number made her suddenly feel immune to the conflict in the house.

Their arguments took Jay back to one day in particular. She was nine years old, and Sammy was seven. Her parents were arguing, her dad trying to keep his voice down, unaware that kids hear everything no matter how quietly parents speak. They wanted to watch the TV, but the signal was intermittent, so Jay sat next to it and wiggled the aerial to get the picture to settle. That was when she heard her dad's muttering and turned to ask him to be quiet, only to see that his lips were sealed. Yet his words continued. *I won't rise to it. Not this time. I won't let her wind me up. It's not my fault you're like this.*

Then she heard her mum, swearing, bristling with anger, the words pinging around her head like angry bees. Jay screamed and clamped her hands to her ears. She ran upstairs to her loft bedroom where she leaned out of the big Velux window and gulped the fresh sea air. She tried to focus, to read her dad's thoughts again, but couldn't figure the mechanism. She even tried a metal coat hanger from her wardrobe and held it in the air, twisting it around. When her dad came to her room a moment later, she looked him in the eye, trying to read him.

A picture formed in Jay's mind, a simple image of feeling – a sense of warmth and concern. Oranges and greens, swirls, curves and waves of colour. Her dad stood in her room frowning at her, but before he said any words the colours changed and she saw that he knew about the power. He had it too.

'Keep it to yourself,' he whispered.

'It's beautiful!' Jay said.

'Yes, it is. It's a gift. But you have to be careful.' He put a finger to his lips.

Sonia's raised voice dragged Jay from her memory. 'Give it a bash,' her mum shouted at Ben, frustrated at the quality of the picture on the television.

'It doesn't help by hitting it,' Ben replied as he tried to keep from raising his voice. Sammy stiffened and Jay caught his eye and tried to reassure him with a stiff smile.

'Then use your powers, see if they'll fix the TV, if they're good for anything useful,' Sonia said, forking spaghetti into her mouth. Ben stopped and looked at her. Then at Sammy. He'd not spoken to Sammy about the powers, only Jay. Sammy knew of course, it just wasn't something that anyone brought up in conversation. 'What?' Sonia asked, mocking innocence.

'Don't,' said Ben.

'I just can't see the point if you don't use them for the benefit of the family,' she said. 'They're pathetic. Can they pay the mortgage? Fix the car? The TV? No. What a waste. Thank god no one else in this family has been blessed with this "power".' She flashed air quotes as she said the word 'power', drawing out the word with a sneer.

Ben lowered his head, staring into his dinner. Sammy stood to fiddle with the aerial on the TV, turning it until the picture improved. Sonia laughed, 'There you go, Ben. That's *power*. Thanks Sammy, love.'

The room was cold, and though filled with people it felt hollow and empty.

Jay looked at the television as she swallowed her dinner as fast as possible. On the screen, a news reporter, on location, shouted to be heard above a chanting crowd. Sonia mumbled something about the unnecessary protest developing. The BBC News programme was following an escalating crisis outside Downing Street.

'That's a lot of people,' said Jay, a slight shiver at the thought of being stuck in the middle of such a crowd, unable to move.

'Thousands,' said Ben. 'They've been gathering all day. They marched through St James's Park and now they're massing all along Whitehall by the looks of it.'

'What are they protesting?' asked Sammy.

'Nothing better to do,' Sonia said, without looking up, but Jay could see that this was no ordinary protest. A tiny spark of static passed between Jay and her dad – his anticipation meeting with her own.

The police had gathered in numbers behind the gates

that sealed off the approach to the Prime Minister's residence. On the other side of the gate was a crowd of angry looking protesters. Jay leaned closer to the television. The aggression in the faces of the protesters unsettled her. A group of police on horseback moved up Whitehall.

'Who's that?' said Jay, motioning towards a striking-looking woman caught on camera at the front of the crowd. The way the crowd moved around her it was clear she was important. She punched the air and then pointed and shouted at the police on the front line at the other side of the gates. 'She's angry.'

'That's Zadie Lawrence,' said Ben, almost a whisper. Jay had heard Zadie's name before. She was a defender of the rights of the gifted. The BBC camera remained focused on Zadie Lawrence as she railed at the police, barring the way through to Downing Street. Jay saw the energy flow from her, shooting from her body like flares. Her passion caught Jay's breath. It sparked something inside of her. She put a hand on her dad's arm, 'We're on her side, right?'

'No,' snapped Sonia.

'Why not?' Ben said. 'She speaks for the oppressed. All kinds of oppressed, not just the Given.'

'She's an extremist,' said Sonia. Jay sensed her dad's pulse quicken, then ease as he took a deep breath. His colours were mixed.

The cameras scanned the protesters. A woman in a red dress with long dreadlocks blew a whistle as she bounced up and down in the crowd. A man held a sign that said *Diversity is Power*. Four young men pushed a police officer who held up his plastic riot shield. Amongst the chaos stood Zadie Lawrence, her arms folded, her eyes nearly closed. Her face was still, an image of peace. While the BBC journalist estimated crowd size, the camera stayed on Zadie.

Suddenly, the line of police guarding Downing Street dropped their shields and began to step backwards. Their arms hung slack, their heads drooped forward. They shuffled until they had revealed the entrance to Downing Street, unguarded. The commentator fell silent as the crowd surged, pouring through the gate and on towards Number Ten. There were more police on horseback, and teams in riot gear with shields and batons. They manoeuvred around the protestors, their shields forming a wall.

Jay sensed the atmosphere as if she were there in person. Aggression hung in the air like a flammable gas cloud waiting for a spark. Ben stood to get closer to the television, leaving his food at the table.

Two police officers at the fringe of the main protest beat a man with their batons as he tried to get away. A police horse barged another into the side of a building, before collapsing on the floor. The camera returned to Zadie Lawrence as she was approached by a line of police.

Jay saw Zadie's colours turn black. 'Dad?' Jay said, her voice trembling. Ben reached across the table and took her hand.

The riot police led a tall man dressed all in black towards Zadie. 'What's happening?' said Jay. 'I don't like this.'

As the police reached Zadie, two of them launched at her with their batons. She went down after the first blow but they continued to beat her. Jay wanted to avert her eyes but couldn't. When the police stopped hitting Zadie, the plain-clothed man approached, crouched and seemed to whisper something in her ear before drawing back. He was doing something to Zadie Lawrence; a dark terrible energy passed from him through her, reducing her in front of the cameras on national television.

Ben looked at Jay, his mouth open and disbelief in his eyes, then back to the screen as Zadie writhed on the floor, her hands clasped to the sides of her head. The man in black stood and nodded to the police officers who reached and pulled Zadie up, dragging her away by her arms, her legs dragging lifelessly along the floor behind her.

Jay glanced at her dad, his eyes fixed on the television, anguish in his expression like she'd never seen before. She turned back to the television as Zadie Lawrence was pushed towards the back of a police van. She'd regained consciousness but was unable to stand.

Just before they pushed her into the van, Zadie Lawrence turned, blood pouring down the side of her face, and looked squarely into the television camera. Jay's world stopped. She felt a bolt of energy and resolve course through her. It was like Zadie Lawrence had looked directly into Jay's mind.

2

I t was the last day of term. Exams had finished and Jay sat in her classroom observing her classmates as though they were primates in a zoo enclosure. Tick by slow tick the clock wound down the seconds until the end of the day. She glanced at the door. Mr Sparks was late. Any minute now people would begin walking out. She turned to Cassie. 'We could leave?'

Cassie flicked her beaded braids out of her eyes. 'What about *him*?' she said. She nodded at Stitch, exchanging banter with the football gang. Every once in a while Stitch would forget that he wasn't the same species as those boys.

Jay shrugged. 'Take him with us?'

Two of the boys from the football team, Jason and Gavin, were becoming agitated with Stitch. They were edgy, hacked off at being inside, nowhere to run around and get rid of their pent up energy.

Jay checked her wrist for the tenth time that day. Nothing. Not even a smudge of a mark. She'd turned eighteen over a week ago and still, no mark.

'Nothing?' said Cassie.

Jay shook her head. 'Nope. You?'

'Nah,' Cassie shrugged but neither of them were surprised about that. Neither Stitch nor Cassie expected anything since they'd not sensed any power. In fact, no one they knew in their class had a mark. Stitch would have loved to have some level of power, even just a level *one* appearing on his wrist would make his year.

Still no sign of Mr Sparks, and now Jason and Gavin looked like they were about to get more serious. Jay eyed them nervously and packed her books into her bag. 'We should go.'

'Might be too late.' Cassie stood. Two of the other football boys had joined in, heckling Stitch and tossing his notebook back and forth over his head. Stitch turned and gave Jay and Cassie a look that clearly said *help me out here, OK?*

Cassie took a step towards Stitch, but Jay put a hand on her arm. Cassie had a brown belt; Jay knew she was more than capable of dealing with a handful of boys. 'Wait a minute. There's something I want to try.'

Jay leaned back in her chair. She closed her eyes, tuning in to Stitch. Focusing had been coming much more naturally to her, but she still had to work at it. With a deep breath she entered her friend's mind. She saw that his outward calm betrayed an inner fear. His pulse raced. She sensed the heat on the surface of his skin, the invisible tears forming in the corners of his eyes, his pain. He wanted to walk away but couldn't find the courage to move.

Jay opened her eyes and looked to Cassie. 'He needs a little help,' she said. Cassie made to stand again but Jay shook her head. 'Let me do it.'

Jason was the most aggressive of the four boys circling Stitch. He kept bouncing up on his toes, puffing his chest out. Jay glanced around the room to make sure no one was looking, then closed her eyes once more to focus in on Jason. His mind was a wide-open and empty space, the colours barely visible before his thoughts streamed through without resistance. He felt excitement mixed with anxiety. As he laughed with his friends at Stitch's expense he felt fear and doubt. Jay left his conscious mind, pushing and prodding a channel into Jason's subconscious, diving into his instincts, his reflexes.

As Jay crept around the edge of Jason's unconscious mind, he kicked out at Stitch's foot like he was warming himself up, testing the water. Cassie twitched in her seat, itching to jump up and defend her friend. But she waited. Jason's aggression came through stronger to Jay, sweeping over her as a mix of excitement and fear. He was preparing to impress his friends. The layers of emotion in Jason revealed a vulnerability and opened a door for Jay. She pierced the outer shell of his consciousness and felt a flash of pride. This was the first time she'd managed this with such clarity. The colours and words came like a burst dam, too much for Jay at first as she rocked back in her chair with the force of it. The stream settled to a steady flow, and the colours merged to a thick, sludgy brown.

She filtered and guided Jason's energy, pushing her own influence into his mind, eventually finding what she was searching for, what she thought might be possible but had never before achieved. Then she squeezed and pushed.

Jay opened her eyes and saw Jason step back from Stitch, almost as if fearing him. He looked down at himself to see a dark patch appear at the front of his trousers. His jaw dropped as the patch spread and stretched down his leg. Jay stared, disbelieving. Cassie gave Jay a sideways look, wide-eyed. Jason's friends backed away from him, their mouths open. A smattering of laughter rose from the class as more people noticed. Then the entire class erupted. People stood and pointed before Jason ran from the room.

Jay and Cassie joined Stitch at the doorway.

'Was that you?' asked Stitch, his face beaming with unfailing devotion.

'I wasn't sure I'd be able to do that,' Jay said. She searched Stitch's reaction for any hint of shame, of disappointment in her for taking it too far. She got nothing. Just usual Stitch, adoring. 'Bit of a moment for me, that was,' she said with a smile.

'Couldn't have happened to a nicer bloke,' said Stitch.

'I didn't know that was possible,' said Cassie.

Jay shrugged. 'Nor me.'

Out front, Jay stopped for a moment and stood at the gates with her back to the college building. On the chalk Downs in the distance, the ring of trees on the ancient hill at Chanctonbury was visible and she could sense the energy. It came in pulses, like a heartbeat. With a little focus, the energy was visible, flowing in waves of colour over the hills towards them and spinning off into the trees and the sky.

'Can you feel it?' said Cassie, standing tall at Jay's side.

'What?' said Stitch.

'Freedom,' said Cassie, grinning. 'No more college.'

She skipped ahead. Jay and Stitch followed and the three friends headed towards Jay's house, away from college for the last time. Stitch reached into the inside pocket of his trademark Oxfam suit jacket and pulled out a packet of tailormade cigarettes, not his usual rolling tobacco.

'Special occasion?' said Jay.

Stitch grinned and planted a cigarette between his teeth. 'After that performance with Jason.'

'I've been feeling it,' said Jay, 'especially since my eighteenth. The power is growing, you know?'

'Nope,' said Stitch, catching her eye as he lit his cigarette. He could read her. As far as Jay could tell, he had no power, except that he had an intuition with her. Most would see it as nothing more than expected between two people who'd been friends for years, but Jay sensed he had something more.

'What's up?' asked Stitch. 'You seem... unsettled.'

Since she'd woken that morning, the air smelled acidic. The wind in the trees sounded ragged. Jay pulled back her sleeve to look for a sign – a smudge, a smear of darkness, anything. Stitch smiled and pulled back his own sleeve to expose bare skin. Jay threw an arm around Stitch's shoulder and took a last look up at the view of Chanctonbury before they turned the corner and into South Street.

3

J ay led her friends to the little bookshop on the corner. Cassie and Stitch both groaned as she made for the door. 'Five minutes,' she said with pleading eyes as she backed in through the door, the bell ringing to alert Alf Harvey to their arrival.

Stitch headed straight to the back room, to sci-fi and fantasy, Cassie following. Jay pulled a book from her bag to return. Alf looked at her over his glasses, a half smile that left creases around his eyes. He picked up the book, read its title, then slipped it beneath the counter.

The bookshop was formed of two town houses knocked together, the top floor a long loft room dedicated to non-fiction. Jay found a table in her favourite quiet corner with the window overlooking the high street. She dumped her bag and jumper and made her way to the rows of shelves allocated to the Given, breathing in the comforting musty smell of the older books as she slipped through the aisles.

The books and records may have been selective, but they were at least free of the sometimes-twisted perspective that came through the television. Books on the Given weren't normally available for loans, and people had to sign in just to read some of them, but Alf never bothered with Jay. He barely even spoke to her. She sensed he might have power, but it was weak, or he was good at shielding. She figured it was best if she kept her distance from him, and he seemed to be content to allow Jay access to the books she wanted without bothering her. He sometimes even let her take books home.

She made straight for the big encyclopaedias on the bottom shelf. These were the oldest reference books on the Given and not available for open access. She carried two volumes back to her table, then returned to the shelves to pick up an autobiography she'd been dipping into on recent visits.

Sasha Colden was the first Given with significant abilities publicly recognised. Her power had been strong. She had more than the ability to *read* minds, she could also influence and control actions by planting thoughts and suggestions. It was Colden's book that seeded the idea in Jay to dig into the subconscious. Sasha had died before she reached her 40th birthday. Jay couldn't find out how she died, but she wasn't surprised. People with power sometimes simply disappeared.

There was a subtext to Sasha's book that Jay was tuning into. On the surface, the pages depicted a life of discovery, of the dangers and opportunities inherent in power, of a life in the public eye, as the first celebrity Given. Sasha was a woman with two lives. Her private family life was not in the pages of her book. Even her actual name was unknown, only her public persona as Colden.

Sasha's openness had encouraged others to self-declare, to join in the growing excitement around the possibilities of life with powers. But in between the lines of her story, another story was hidden.

There was a creak on the stairs. Jay glanced up to catch Alf Harvey staring at her. They held eye contact for a moment before he looked away, then mounted the final stair before turning to flick through records in the filing cabinet next to the stairwell. Alf often came up to the top floor when Jay was there, and more than once Jay felt that he was keeping an eye on her. Jay picked a couple of books at random from the nearest shelf, the authorised books, and placed them over the encyclopaedias.

She closed the Sasha Colden book and pulled one of the old encyclopaedias towards her, careful to position the other books so Alf Harvey wouldn't see what she was reading. She opened the encyclopaedia at a page she'd bookmarked before, on the modern history of the powers. This was the period before she was born, before the world turned against the Given. Powers had been suspected for centuries, but only verified through tests for the first time less than fifty years ago. People with powers had been treated like royalty back then, holding positions of influence all over the world.

Jay felt the bookseller's presence before he spoke. 'Up here again?' he said.

Jay flinched. They'd never made chit chat before. She looked up at him. Colours seeped from the man like visible gas leaking from the crevices in a rock face. His tones were smooth, his colours neutral, revealing nothing of his intentions. Jay could spot danger in the darkness of people's colours, or openness in the yellows and greens. With Alf Harvey, the colours were a mixture, almost as if he were consciously concealing. And there was something more. The wisps of colour were constrained like she'd not seen before. Most people's colours presented to Jay without ambiguity, but Alfred's flowed for a moment and then disappeared as if sucked up with a powerful vacuum cleaner. The colours were gone before any words could come that Jay could read.

He was an effective shielder. She'd never seen anyone hide so completely. He left no cracks, nothing but a smooth deflection. Her attempts to read him revealed nothing, and he knew it. She locked eyes with him again and he gave a satisfied, crooked smile that sent a shiver through her bones.

Alf Harvey glanced over his shoulder towards the stairs. 'You need to be careful. Especially in here,' he said.

The muscles in Jay's body tightened, 'Sorry, Mr Harvey,' she said, her voice weak. She gathered her things, closing the encyclopaedia and concealing it with another book. She stood to leave. He knew too much. She had done everything her dad had taught her not to do – she'd been careless.

He took the seat opposite her. 'Hold on, dear. It's OK. And call me Alf.' The soft tone of his voice dispersed some tension in Jay. She stopped packing her things and looked around the room. They were alone.

'It's easy enough to tell by your reading what your interests are,' he said.

Jay shrugged.

'How long have you known?'

'Known what?' Jay said. Alf smiled, and they were silent for a minute.

'OK,' Jay said, 'so what if I have it?' The tightness in her muscles returned. But she wanted to talk, wanted *him* to talk. With a mix of fear and excitement she ached to speak about the powers with someone who understood. She'd talked to Stitch, of course, her best friend since they were small, and to Cassie. Stitch knew all about the Given, the legend and the powers, but not from the inside, not from feeling it, only from studying it.

Alf settled in his seat. 'You need to be careful. We have Scanners who come in here most days, trying to weed out the resistance.'

'What resistance?' Jay asked. She'd heard of the Scanners before, a word used for people with power who worked for the State, scanning to detect other people illegally using their abilities.

Alf smiled. 'Just keep your head down. Things are a little hotter than usual at the moment, since the protest.'

He turned at the sound of footsteps to see Cassie and Stitch emerge from the stairwell. He stood. 'I'd better head back down, remember what I said.'

4

Into the Beach Lane estate, Stitch lagged behind as Cassie quizzed Jay on why she'd been speaking to Alf.

'You know he's senile, right?' Cassie said.

'He's not, he's OK,' said Jay.

'He talks in riddles,' said Cassie.

They crossed the road and almost bumped into a group of boys walking in the opposite direction. Cassie turned and ran after them.

'Cassie...' said Jay. But she'd already caught up with the tallest of the three boys and spun him around. The boy turned and stared at her.

'Sorry.' Cassie dropped her head and ran back to Jay and Stitch.

For a moment no one spoke. Then Stitch asked quietly, 'You thought it was Reuben?'

Cassie sighed.

'You still think about him a lot, huh?' Jay said, gently.

Cassie shrugged. 'That bloke just looked so...' She trailed off.

Jay linked her arm in Cassie's. 'Still gets to you?' she said.

Cassie nodded. 'Just when I think I've got him out of my system, something like that happens.'

'Where did he go? You never told us.'

Cassie looked down at Jay, smiling. 'All I know is what my grandad said, that his family moved away, up north. He knew Reuben's parents. Then we lost Grandad too, so I never had time to ask him about it. But moving away is not a reason to go completely dark. Not a word. No letter, nothing.'

* * *

JAY PUSHED OPEN her front door. When Stitch saw Sammy he held up a hand for a high five. Jay's little brother was just sixteen and already stood a good six inches taller than Jay. He'd always been tall, came out of the womb all gangly and awkward.

Sammy's cheeks flushed as Cassie enveloped him in a hug. Jay wasn't sure if there was a chemistry between them or if it was just Cassie's sheer beauty that knocked her little brother off kilter. Cassie gave him a wink as she pulled away and ruffled his hair.

Jay looked up at her brother. 'We're going up, come if you want?'

Sammy glanced at Cassie and hesitated a moment before he said, 'I'm out, meeting the others, last day and all that. We have some celebrating to do.' He grinned. Jay figured they'd be marking the end of school by working their way through a few cans down on the beach.

The presence of her friends filled Jay's small loft bedroom. Posters on the walls overlapped where she'd bought new ones and not bothered to remove the old. Her dad's old hi-fi separates had made their way into her room, topped by his turntable now in pride of place. Stitch sat in his favourite spot on the floor under the big Velux window and took out his cigarettes. Cassie picked out a few records and passed them to Stitch.

Stitch said, 'So what did Alf have to say?'

'He has power, did you know that?'

Cassie snorted. 'Crazy old man.'

Stitch looked up at Jay. 'He always shows a weird interest in you. He didn't sense your power?'

Jay's head told her to be careful around Alf, like her dad would say, but her heart told her that he was OK, and curiosity said that she'd need to see him again. 'No, I think my secret is safe for now.'

The three friends listened to records and talked about summer plans – debating if they could afford to take the summer without having to find work. Stitch wanted to camp out, live cheap in the hills and woods of the Downs. 'We don't need money,' he said.

'Why camping?' said Cassie. 'We need to *do* something, no point in sitting around on a hill waiting for something to happen.' Stitch opened his mouth to argue then seemed to think better of it.

'We've only just got out of college, what's the rush?' Jay said. Her first thoughts were for exploring her developing power, but in a way that didn't draw attention. Her dad would not be impressed if he sensed her power dispersing into the environment, but she yearned to let it loose. She wondered how long she could even contain it. She looked again at her wrist.

Stitch noticed. 'You need to cut down on wrist inspections. It'll drive you mad. Give it time.'

Cassie stood. 'If you two are getting into spiritual talk again, I'll be off.'

'Tomorrow then?' said Jay. 'We can hang at the beach?' Cassie nodded and slipped out through the Velux window and onto the roof, from where she'd jump down the side, onto the wall by the tree and into the alleyway that led around to her house.

* * *

IT WAS DARK. Spent record sleeves scattered the bed and floor. Stitch made himself comfortable on the bed next to Jay, their backs up against the wall. He was still wearing his suit jacket. He huffed to himself, 'She always bails out when we talk about the powers.'

Jay knew it too. Cassie would switch off if Stitch talked about the energy of the land – the ley lines and the hill forts.

Stitch smiled at Jay and said, 'What's on your mind?'

'Can't you read?'

'Not today. Can't see anything in there, reckon you're hiding something.'

'You remember the legend that my dad used to talk about?'

Stitch nodded. 'The Interland? I loved those stories. My favourite bit of sleepovers.'

Jay remembered how Stitch's eyes would widen and he'd grow silent as soon as her dad began talking. 'We always thought that they were just his stories. Now I'm not so sure. I think there's more to it.'

'What are you getting at?' said Stitch.

'I don't know. This place. It's all connected. The Downs, the ley lines, the hill forts. And maybe the Interland.'

'Probably, but why are you thinking about all this now?'

'Last night. When I got back. I sat out on the roof with Sammy for a while. When he went to bed I opened up a bit.'

'What did you see?'

Jay couldn't remember much. There was something, some activity, more than the usual whispers that she would often hear at night. There was a human connection, something dark, and it left a bitter taste. She must have dropped off to sleep then, her head resting on the roof tiles, because a while later she woke to whispers from the south, from the sea. She'd opened to the sea before, many times. It was like lowering a microphone beneath its surface and eavesdropping on the millions of tiny interactions. Not words. Not even thoughts, but communication, meaning, and feeling. Whispers turned to white noise at first. Then she would try to filter, collect the patterns and tune in to the different threads. But they evaded her, like trying to catch fish with her hands.

'Did you know that fish feel love?' said Jay.

Stitch snorted. 'What?'

'Fish.'

'I thought their brains were so small that their memory span was, like, a few seconds.'

'That's crap. They love deeper than we do.'

'Good to know,' said Stitch.

Back when they were sixteen, on a night much like this one, Jay and Stitch slept together. They'd been friends since they were babies – he was like family. They talked about everything together and this evening they got onto the subject of sex. Neither of them had been with anyone yet. One minute they were laughing and joking about it and the next they were kissing and undressing each other. He stayed over that night. Not like his usual sleepovers when they slept in their clothes, top to tail. On that night they slept with their heads on the same pillow. The first time was supposed to be rubbish, but this first time didn't follow that rule. Jay had connected with Stitch. Deeply. The next day they both kind of agreed, without words, that they'd keep the night to themselves.

'So it's worms *and* fish now?' said Stitch, nodding towards the glass-fronted worm farm that took up a quarter of the far wall. It looked like a grand tropical fish tank except filled with layers of composting material and hundreds of worms.

'Worms are far more callous,' said Jay, smiling. 'Very single-minded, determined little buggers. Not as romantic as fish.'

Stitch laughed and leaned in to Jay so that his head rested on her shoulder. She leaned back into him, resting her own head on top of his. She could smell his hair wax, a fresh, herby scent that was so familiar to her it was like it was her own.

'Sammy ate one once,' said Jay.

'What?' said Stitch.

'A worm. He was about three years old. I was five or six. I came in here and he had one hanging out of his mouth. I pulled the end but the other end was lodged down his throat and it broke in half.'

Stitch laughed. 'My dad would've taken me to hospital for a stomach pump.'

Jay leaned over to lie back on her bed. 'How is your dad?' she asked. Since Stitch's mum had died, back when Stitch was eleven or twelve, his dad had been a little off-piste. He'd thrown himself into his faith and seemed intent on blocking out Stitch.

'No change in his condition, as they say in the ICU.'

'Not sure religion is a condition.'

'Depends on your perspective.' Stitch yawned and

squeezed himself under Jay's covers, fully clothed, so they were top-to-tail.

'Tomorrow,' said Jay. 'What do you think we should do?'

Stitch's breathing deepened and slowed. 'Night then, Stitch.'

Jay cleared away the record sleeves. She found her dad's *Neil Young* LP, pulled it from its sleeve and lowered it onto the turntable before squeezing back under her covers. Beyond her window a light blinked on the horizon, a bonfire up at Highdown. She turned the volume dial on her stereo until Neil Young's voice was low enough not to keep her awake, but loud enough to distract her from her racing thoughts. She lay back on her bed and closed her eyes.

5

A week into summer and still no decisions made. Stitch hadn't been around, saying that he was trying to spend some time at home with his dad. Cassie was fickle as ever, turning up in the middle of the night once, then disappearing for days.

In the lounge, Sammy flicked at the buttons to cycle through the four available channels on the television while Jay read her book, or at least trained her eyes on the words. Ben rested on the sofa, his newspaper balanced on his knee. Sammy's channel-hopping grated on Jay's nerves and her mind wandered. The newspapers said Zadie Lawrence had been imprisoned, but her dad said that he'd heard she'd been killed, along with many others. Jay felt waves of despair and anger that she didn't fully understand, that pulled at her insides.

Sammy gave up flicking through channels. The News programme reported on the success of the government's "home-fires" initiative, their drive to "get back to the roots of British society". Jay watched as Ben's colours darkened. She could feel him worrying that the rising tension and crusade against the Given meant more scrutiny, more chance Jay would be detected.

Jay stood. The room felt too close. The thoughts banging around in her head were too loud. She made for the kitchen and put the kettle on. Ben followed. 'Hey,' he said, 'can you see what's happening?'

'They won't find us,' Jay said.

'They're turning everyone against us, we can't stop it. You heard what they were saying about the Given taking positions of influence, jumping the queues, taking people's jobs. That's the kind of thing that makes people angry.' Ben paced, tapping his fingers along the counter in agitation. 'It's time you understood this.'

'But none of it is true,' Jay said as the kettle boiled.

'It doesn't matter what's true. Jay. Listen. You need to bury it deeper. I've sensed you out on that roof, and if I can see your power, others can too.'

Jay lowered her gaze, unable to maintain eye contact. 'It's not right,' she said, 'the Given have the same rights...'

'The Given don't exist anymore. They've been...'

'*They*?' Jay shouted. 'You mean *us*.'

Jay's dad spoke slowly and deliberately, 'Like I was saying, *they* don't exist. The Given are consigned to history. Imprisoned. Killed. On the run. It's different now; it's not just frowned upon, the powers are illegal. And it's not just here, it's the same in Europe. There have been televised executions in America.'

The kettle clicked off and the bubbling subsided. The room filled with silence. Jay wouldn't allow herself to cry. Nothing useful could come from crying. Yet, tears prickled in the corners of her eyes. 'It's not right...' was all she could say.

Her dad continued, 'They're not stopping at people who

use their power. They're taking anyone that *has* power, whether they're using it or not.'

'Why?'

Ben pulled back his sleeve to show the number two on the inside of his wrist – one of the few times Jay had seen it. 'It's not like we can hide these if someone wants to look. If you give them a reason to come, it's over.' He held her shoulders, 'Do you understand, Jay?'

For the first time in her life, Jay wanted to slap her dad across the face. She was sure that if he referred to the Given as "they" one more time then she wouldn't be able to help herself. Jay wondered again what level she would be, what number would appear on her wrist.

Ben looked over at her wrist. 'Anything showing yet?'

Jay pulled up her left sleeve and shook her head.

'Soon,' he said, sadness passing across his face.

'This crackdown doesn't make sense,' said Jay.

Ben sighed. 'Jake down the club told me that they're recruiting for Readers.' He glanced at Jay. She raised her eyebrows at him and he continued, 'Not the recruitment you might imagine. More of a forced enrolment where the alternative...' He paused. 'Rehab. The *Sub Levels*.'

'So they want high-level recruits? Not like you, and me?'

'Maybe,' Ben said, seeming to sink further into himself. 'There aren't many at the top end though, I imagine they'd take anyone, whatever the level.'

'How many are there at the top levels?' asked Jay.

'Other than Zadie Lawrence, only one other has scored at level eight.'

'Who?' said Jay, thinking about Sasha Colden.

'We're not sure.'

'*We*?'

'I have some friends. Some like us I speak to sometimes...'

'You hypocrite. Who are they?' Jay stiffened, bristling. He *still* treated her as if she were twelve years old, keeping her in the dark, only releasing snippets of information that *he* judged her to be able to deal with. 'Are you a part of the resistance Alf was talking about?'

Ben shook his head. 'Don't listen to that old man. What's he been saying?' Jay shook her head and remained silent. 'It's not a resistance,' Ben said. 'It's just like-minded people. We keep our heads down, attract no attention. It's more like a research group than a resistance these days.'

'Research into what?' She turned away from him and poured water from the kettle into two mugs.

Ben looked at her. 'OK, sit down. You want to know? I'll tell you.' He pushed the kitchen door closed. He picked the milk from the fridge and handed it to her. 'Some of the Given recruited by the authorities went through a transformation process as they became Readers. Their power scaled up. These Readers are dedicated to the purges, using their senses to root out people like us.'

'Scaled up?'

'A level three or four Given is coming out at a six or seven Reader. And they're a nasty bunch, revelling in the State sanctioned power they have. Some of them they call "Scanners", and the more powerful ones are the Readers.'

'So they want to turn us, the Given, into Readers?'

'Maybe. Some of us. But it seems most never re-emerge, so it's only the select few who come out as Readers. The rest of us...' He trailed off. 'They all share one thing – the Scanners and the Readers – they've all accepted the transformation, a one-way ticket. They are no longer part of the Given.'

Jay took a step towards the fridge to scrutinise the

arrangement of the magnetic pieces on the fridge chess board. 'Whose move is it?' The kitchen chess match had lasted a month this time, both Jay and her dad taking their time, sometimes a week between moves.

'Your move.'

Jay slid her black bishop into a better attacking position. Her dad watched as she released her finger from the bishop.

'Bold,' he said.

They were silent for a while. Jay stirred sugar into her tea, her mind racing with thoughts about the Readers, their scaled-up power. She wondered whether Zadie Lawrence was dead, or if she'd become a Reader. She would be one who the State would have loved to see on their side, hunting down the rest of the Given.

Ben gazed out of the kitchen window. 'I suppose you remember the legend?' he said.

Jay knew her dad's stories well, from the years of bedtime narrations transfixing her and Sammy, and sometimes Stitch too, for hours. His fiction depicted a far off land, a magical oasis and a source of power. He made a connection between his stories and the words of a myth, an ancient legend.

'You remember, right?' Ben said.

'Kind of.' Jay handed him a mug of tea and waited. He reached for the fridge and moved his magnetic pawn to block the attack from Jay's bishop. He pulled himself up to sit on the kitchen worktop, legs hanging over the side. Jay stood on the opposite side of the narrow galley kitchen and cradled her tea as her dad began his interpretation of the legend.

6

The legend has no fixed point in history. It simply always was, and was handed down through generations. Most people who relayed the story did so by placing it in the context of their own culture, their own country. Even its written versions differed, from tales of hidden islands in the middle of the ocean, to magical portals atop mountains leading to other lands.

Ben insisted that the original source of the story was written into the myths and folklore. 'The parallels are too much to ignore,' he said, 'between the words in the written folklore of the South Downs and what we know of the legend.'

'No one else seems to think so, Dad,' Jay said, smiling with affection, remembering the enthusiasm and joy he would take in embellishing the story a little more every night at bedtime.

'Have you read the folklore?'

Jay nodded. 'Some of it. Compared to your bedtime stories it's about as exciting as reading an instruction manual.'

Ben laughed. 'Well that's fair. There are clues in the folk-lore, but there are missing pieces.' He lowered his voice. 'Pieces only visible to some people, not everyone.'

Jay snorted. 'Come on, Dad. Seriously?'

'I know it sounds odd. And I'm not saying that I have all the answers, but from what we can tell, the pieces fall into place only for those who need it.'

'Need it for what?' Jay asked.

Ben looked up at Jay. He held out his hand.

'What?' said Jay.

'Let me touch your hand, I want to try something.'

Jay gave a nervous smile, wondering if her dad was going crazy. She held out her hand and Ben placed his on top. He closed his eyes and Jay felt something. It was nothing unusual to connect with her dad, even without touching, but this was different; it came from inside her. A flash of light behind her eyes. Another, brighter this time. Images floated through her mind and she too closed her eyes. The images were just beyond her reach, too distant to grasp, to interpret or to understand. Another flash, a clearer picture this time – an oasis of light, a pool and a cave with water flowing. Then darkness.

Jay withdrew her hand. Ben opened his eyes and shook his head. 'Sorry. I can't get it.'

'What was that?' said Jay, breathless, jumping up to pace the room.

'I think there's a way we can transmit information faster through touch. I had hoped I might impart what I know, all of it, not simply what I'm able to articulate. I don't think I have the information in any decipherable form in my mind. And my power is not strong enough to transmit properly, anyway.'

'I got something. But how did you...'

'Someone did it to me. A long time ago.'

'Who?' Jay continued to pace the kitchen, her mind turning and twisting over what she'd seen through her dad's touch. 'And why?' she said.

'I don't even know if it's possible to transmit information like that. It's just a feeling. It was so long ago it's like it was a dream.'

Jay shook her head as if trying to dislodge something. The image of a pool and interconnected caves swam through her mind. Her eyes wide, she said, 'Tell me what else you've figured out about the legend?' Jay had thought she knew as much as her dad, but now she wasn't so sure, and she'd had enough of his selective truth.

Ben pulled a notebook from the back pocket of his jeans and flicked through pages of hand-written words and pencil sketches. He closed it again. 'If this place is the source, then the Readers would be keen to find it. Even if just to destroy it. Without the source, the Given are powerless and the job of the Readers is done.' Jay nodded.

Ben lowered his gaze. 'As much as we might want to find this place, we wouldn't want to be the ones to lead the Readers there.'

Jay waited. Her dad looked at her. 'And the state is aware of our group. They're actively looking for us, might even be watching.'

'Your *resistance* group?'

Ben smiled. 'You might call it that.' He jumped down off the kitchen surface and moved his magnetic queen to take Jay's bishop, ending her attack.

7

I nside the circle of trees atop Chanctonbury Hill, Marcus gritted his teeth and whittled a stick to within a millimetre of its life, the blade of his knife glinting in the glow of embers from the fire. Smoke rose and dissolved into the night above his head.

He sucked air between his clenched teeth. In the time before he had become a Reader, back when he was one of the Given, Chanctonbury would have been a source of power – up there he would have been like a battery placed on a charger. Not anymore. Now, Marcus felt nothing. His power came from a different place, somewhere controlled not by the energy of the land, but by the State.

He stopped with his knife and kicked a log into the fire. Flames illuminated his face. His skin was weathered, the dark rings around his eyes accentuated by the shadows, and the scar on his face silvery in the light of the flames. A black mark on the inside of his left wrist displayed the number eight.

The hill at Chanctonbury was steeped in layers of history, layers that had each charged the ground with energy. Myth said that the Devil himself created the Hill as he dug the ground for the valley that formed Devil's Dyke, discarding a clump of earth from his spade onto the Downs. The ring of trees at Chanctonbury, like those at nearby Cissbury and Highdown, were visible from as far as the coast in the south, and from the top of the Downs to the north.

A grey squirrel scampered up a tree to a vantage point halfway up, scanning the clearing, an eye on the man with the knife who seemed to shimmer in the light of the fire. Marcus pulled back his sleeve with his knife, tracing the curves of the figure eight, a mark that, before his transformation, had been a figure six.

As if coming in on a breeze, a flash of an image crossed his mind. He was alert, scanning. It was an unknown power signature. Someone new. Someone with power who had so far evaded the authorities, perhaps someone who had now come of age, and come up for air. Their signal was intense, but disturbed, intermittent. The image came again, smeared into his consciousness, a smudge of light and colour. A figure. A silhouette. A voice. All of it fleeting, too momentary to absorb. But something familiar... something from his past.

'Who...' Marcus said aloud, a rising anger in his chest. This new energy was a personal attack. Someone had evaded him, he who was convinced that the world of the powers belonged only to him. He had earned his place. It had been that way since he accepted the mandate handed to him by the State. In the so-called *choice* – the option of life as a Reader over that of a slow diminution of power – he chose life. He had the facial scar to show for it, a mark inflicted by the channelling of substantial power into him, turning him, releasing him.

He dropped his stick into the fire, stood, and looked over

his shoulder to the south, his mind open. Another image, a piercing flash this time, crashed into his head like an angry scream.

'Who *is* this?' He wandered towards the edge of the ring of trees, pain piercing his temples, eyes watering. He tilted his head as if to hear more clearly and looked out over the trees towards the coast.

He smiled. Someone with power had strayed into his zone of perception. They were in him now. He had their scent.

8

Sammy scattered the chess pieces over the carpet. 'Black or white?' he said.

'White,' said his dad.

Sammy smiled. 'I'll be white. White goes first.'

Sonia was on the sofa, her head in a magazine. She looked towards the front door, then at her watch as if waiting for something. Jay had been upstairs for most of the morning, her loft room becoming more like her own separate residence, with her own front door via the roof and the Velux window.

'Your go.' Sammy had made his signature opening move, his classic queen's knight offensive. 'Prepare to defend,' he said.

Ben smiled, pleased things seemed to have returned to something like normal. They had reached an equilibrium. There was less coverage of the Given on the television and in the news. Occasionally, there would be whispers of an incident, someone causing a problem for the authorities, but these incidents became rarer, and talk of them less animated, less credible even.

Sammy brought out his second knight. As Ben considered his defence a sudden wave of nausea hit him. It was as if the wind had been knocked out of him. He looked up at Sonia. 'What?' she said. 'Seen a ghost?'

Ben tuned back to Sammy but he couldn't concentrate. Another pang of nausea shot through him and he jerked his hand to his mouth. 'Sorry, Sammy. I'll be back in a minute.'

'I'll take your go,' said Sammy.

Ben lurched to the downstairs toilet where he leaned over the basin, sweat beading on his forehead. The nausea subsided a little, and he splashed cold water on his face. 'There's a Reader coming,' he said to himself as he dried his face. 'They've found me.'

He threw the towel onto the floor and opened the toilet door in a single move then bounded up the stairs three at a time. 'Jay?' he shouted, stepping towards the open Velux window.

'Hey, Dad.' She poked her head through. 'What's up?'

'Did you feel it?'

'What?' Jay thought for a moment. 'I did sense something. Was that you?'

'Someone's coming,' Ben said.

'Who?'

'One of the government's Readers. A nasty one.'

'It's OK. We can shield. Just close-up. He won't find us.'

'He already has.' As Ben said these words, there was an urgent banging on their front door. They stared at each other, neither moving. 'Stay there, close the window behind you and shield.'

'I'll come...'

'Stay! Please. Stay. We don't know how strong this one is.'

Ben's heart thumped and his skin prickled as he headed back to the stairs, pausing on the top step. He heard Sammy talking to a man at the front door. He summoned all his strength to create as much confusion in the energy as he could, hoping it might shield Jay. His shielding skills were not great, not as good as his ability to sense others with power. The best he could hope for was creating enough confusion for the Reader to think that he was the only one in the house with power. What wasn't clear was whether it was Jay that the Reader had come for, or if it was him. He cursed himself at how stupid he'd been. His resistance work. Careless.

A wave of energy swept through the house, up the stairs and through his body. He almost fell back onto the stairs. This one was scanning with a force he'd not experienced before. His heart raced and his face flushed with the effort of maintaining his shield. He took a moment to compose himself before continuing down the stairs.

'Can I help you?' Ben asked.

The unshaven man looked up.

'This is Mr Jimmy. For you,' Sammy said, and turned to head back to the lounge. 'Don't be long, it's your move.'

'Mr Jimmy?' He was a good ten inches shorter than Ben but he was stocky, almost as wide as he was tall. His three-quarter length jacket looked more like a trench coat.

'Just call me Jimmy,' the man said, looking into Ben's eyes. He held out his identification. Ben glanced at it but he already knew who this man was, *what* he was. As he put his ID badge away, Ben caught sight of the number six on the inside of his wrist. He tried not to think about it, not to leave thoughts in his head that the man could read – he wouldn't stand a chance facing up to a level six.

'And if I have it right,' the man said, 'you must be Ben?'

'What can I do for you?' said Ben. 'We're just in the middle of something.'

'Chess, your boy said. Lovely.' His self-satisfied smile revealed nicotine-stained teeth. 'I've been looking for you.'

'What for?'

'You've been leaking signals for a while now but we couldn't triangulate. Something was blocking. Marcus reckoned it was probably all the bloody ley lines in these parts. It's crazy around here.'

'Marcus?'

'Oh, sorry. Marcus is the boss.'

Ben glanced over Jimmy's shoulder to see if there was a second Reader outside. Ben had heard the name Marcus before, in connection with the fabled level eight, the strongest government reader.

'He's not here, just me,' said Jimmy. 'So what level are you?'

'Level?' Ben was twitchy, like a caged bird.

'Stay with me, Ben. What level are you? Let me see your wrist.'

Ben hiked his sleeve to show his mark.

'Two?' said Jimmy, sounding disappointed. 'I'm surprised.'

'About what?'

'Marcus said you'd be a four or five and that I should bring someone else with me.'

Ben breathed a sigh of resignation. 'So, what now?'

'Perhaps I can come in and we can have a talk? I'd like to hear about your little group. I hear it's growing by the day and there must be a long list of names you're dying to give me?'

'No. If you want to talk, we can do it here.'

A flash of annoyance shot from Jimmy. 'You need to pack a little bag, not too much, and then you need to say your goodbyes. Bring your membership lists or we will just have to come back again and rip everything apart until we find it for ourselves. Come out to the vehicle. You've got five minutes. Don't think about it, just do it. If you try to run, I'll cause you pain. If you take longer than five minutes, I'll cause your wife pain too. If you do anything stupid, like try to take me on, then I'll cause pain to all three of you, and I'll pay particular attention to the boy.'

All three of us. Ben took a deep breath and reinforced his shield. 'Five minutes,' Ben said. He knew that Jimmy meant business, and he knew about the ability of the higher level readers to cause pain through the concentration of thoughts, pain that could debilitate, and, at its worst, cause lasting damage.

The man turned and made his way back to his Land Rover. Ben closed the door then called out for Sammy to come upstairs. He turned and ran up to Jay's room. The longer the Reader was out there, the more likely he'd sense something of Jay.

As Ben climbed awkwardly through Jay's Velux window, she had her eyes closed. 'Hey,' said Ben.

She breathed out. 'Has he gone?'

'Keep shielding.'

'He's still out there?'

'Yes. Can you shield us both?'

'But we're OK, right?'

Sammy appeared at the window. 'What is it?'

'Come out here. I want to talk to you both, I don't have long.' He smiled as Sammy scrambled out of the window and settled next to him. He put an arm around each of his children.

'What do you mean you don't have long?' said Jay.

Ben didn't answer, turned to Sammy. 'You've heard of the Given, right?'

'I know about your powers, Dad, and Jay's.'

'You what?' Ben started.

'I told him,' said Jay, impatient. 'Tell us, Dad. What is it?'

'That man at the door,' said Ben, looking at Sammy and sensing a rising tide of emotion in his son that was about to spill out. Sammy was a special boy. He had no power that Ben could tell, but he had *something*. He was sensitive, that was true, probably too sensitive. He experienced people's emotions and their troubles as if they were his own. He was intuitive, and he was kind.

'Jimmy?' asked Sammy.

'Yes. He's a Reader. You know what that is?'

Sammy nodded and Jay lowered her head into her hands. 'He detected you.' she said.

Ben put a hand on Jay's arm. 'Listen. We don't have much time. He wants a list of people in my group. I've got five minutes to bring it out front. If I don't, then...' He looked up at the view of the hills. He took a deep breath, taking in as much as he could, not knowing when he'd next be able to feel the energy of the Downs. 'If I don't, then he won't hold back. And he won't stop at me. If he returns, he'll detect you too, Jay. I can't let that happen.'

'Just give him the list. He might let you stay?'

'I don't have a list. There is no such list. But either way, they want me too, not just the list.'

Jay was wide-eyed, pleading, searching for a solution. 'I might be stronger than him. We can try...'

'No, Jay. He's a level six.' Ben looked away, wanting to hold Jay tight and not let go, but he needed to be strong so that *she* could be strong, for Sammy. They would have to survive without him.

'Where will they take you, Dad?' said Sammy.

'A holding camp I expect.'

'Prison,' Jay said. 'Don't dress it up. They'll put you in prison, or *rehabilitation* as they call it.' A realisation showed in Jay's eyes. 'Will they try to transform you?'

Ben shook his head. 'They won't bother with me.' He tried to pull her closer, but Jay resisted, pushing herself away from him. She shoved her hand hard against his chest. He didn't try to stop her.

'I'm sorry,' he said, then opened out his arm and pulled in Sammy.

'Look, we knew this was always a possibility.'

'Then *do* something. Fight. Do *anything*,' Jay screamed, her face a mass of tears and anger.

Ben pulled her close, using his strength to force her to settle, smothering her screams so the Reader wouldn't hear them. 'Shush,' he said in a stern tone, no time for patience. 'You need to grow up. This could be you. This is serious.'

Jay's struggles gradually subsided. 'What now?'

'We need to think about this as a step on the journey. It might not be the one we'd planned, but we can deal with it.'

'What journey?' said Sammy.

'Our journey. The journey through life. There are always challenges; it's how we deal with them that determines who we are.'

Sammy rubbed his eyes, holding back tears. Jay leaned in closer to Ben. 'They'll come for me too?' she said.

'Not if you're careful. Right now, he doesn't know you're here. More than ever you need to bury it. Shield. Never let your guard down.' Ben took Jay by the shoulders and gently shook her until she met his eyes. 'Give them nothing to go on.'

Jay wanted to be brave but the shudder of a sob passed through her as she looked into her father's eyes. 'We'll never be properly free,' she said.

PART II

POWERS

9

J ay's lungs burned as she pushed herself to keep running. She couldn't shake the feeling that if she slowed, a Reader would be behind her, getting closer. Her father was gone, and it was all her fault. All Jay could think to do was to head to the bookshop and talk to Alf.

She slammed into the door and fell into the shop. 'Alf,' she said, leaning on the counter to keep herself from collapsing onto the floor.

'Jay?' Alf raised an eyebrow, exhibiting no real sense of urgency. 'Back so soon, my girl.'

'They took my dad,' she spluttered, snapping Alf from his serenity.

He said nothing but nodded towards the stairs, his expression neutral and demeanour calm. Colours drifted from him as he looked at Jay – soothing greens and yellows. He made for the stairs. Jay followed.

'Why did they take him? He's just a level two,' Jay said as they sat at her favourite table.

'They might have sensed you.'

'But I have nothing,' said Jay, motioning towards her wrist.

'Not yet.'

She stood and paced the room, looking out through the windows. She saw a Reader in every person that walked the high street.

Alf leaned back in his chair. 'They'll take everyone eventually, but I agree it's odd that they would take a level two.' He paused, thinking. 'They must have sensed something more powerful.' He held Jay's eye for a moment.

'You really think I'm the reason they took him?'

'I'm not saying anything for sure. I know no more than you, but it's possible. Even I can tell that your power is stronger than almost any I've felt.' He leaned and pulled a book from the shelf behind him, the Sasha Colden biography. He slapped it down on the table. 'Like this woman here.'

Jay nodded. 'She had proper power.'

Alf looked towards the stairs. 'Sasha had more than that.' He touched the book cover. 'She was...'

'What about my dad?' Jay interrupted. 'Where are they taking him?'

Alf nodded for Jay to sit. 'I know it's hard, but there's nothing you can do about it now. What you can do is look after number one, or you will be next. It's important the Readers don't find you.'

Jay felt a tingle travel from her neck down her left arm and settle in her wrist. She shivered. She picked at her sleeve, slowly pulling it back. As her sleeve edged back further she saw the marking, its deep blackness like a hole in her wrist. The curve of the lower section revealed, she looked up at Alf whose eyes remained fixed on her arm. She dragged her sleeve back the rest of the way and the figure of eight was clear. Her heart pounded.

Alf nodded. 'Do you have anywhere you can go?'

'No.' Jay laughed without humour. 'I'm not going anywhere. I can't. I've just finished college. I can't leave my brother.'

'Wait there a minute.' He stood and moved around to the back of the room where he unlocked a cupboard. He returned with a bunch of papers, opening an old, yellowing map on the table in front of Jay. 'This came in a while back. I've not logged it so the Readers don't know about it yet, but I can't leave it too long. They'll suspect something.'

'Where is this place?' said Jay, leaning over the map.

'That's the thing. There are no landmarks. Nothing to locate it. The detail is so generic it could be a thousand places, but look.' He drew Jay's attention to a corner of the map where the topography had been annotated with hand-drawn lines.

'Bows and arrows,' Jay whispered.

Alf looked at her and nodded. 'Like it says in the legend.'

The lines on the map formed the shape of two sets of bow and arrow, with intersecting trajectories, like Ben had described to her. 'But,' Jay stuttered, 'there's nothing here to anchor it. This could be anywhere.' There was no distinguishable coastline, no rivers. 'Anyone could have drawn this, it's just a picture.'

Alf leaned back in his seat. 'Maybe. But it's old for sure. And see here.' He pointed to what looked like clumps of trees. 'This might be Chanctonbury.'

Jay looked closer, 'Or Highdown? Or Cissbury?'

'One of the hill forts,' said Alf.

'Can I take it with me?' said Jay.

Alf shook his head. 'Too dangerous. You take something like this from here, they'll know. Eventually they'll know.' He turned then, looking across to the stairway as a tall man dressed in black stepped up from the stairs and moved towards the window. Alf's face turned grey and Jay sensed his shield begin to show cracks. A shiver crept up her spine, and she saw his fear in colours – a diffusion of dark crimson, almost black it was so deep, expanding into the room like a noxious gas.

'Go,' Alf said.

'Where?'

'Use the back stairs.' He pointed towards a fire escape. Jay held the bookseller's eyes for a moment, deciding whether he was to be trusted, whether those stairs would lead to safety. Through the cracks of his mind, she saw his fear and urgency for her safety, streams of crimson now flowing into a spectrum of yellows.

She grabbed her bag and lunged for the door. A wave of energy shoved at her back. She pushed through to the spiral staircase, looking over her shoulder to catch the eye of the man in black. The door closed behind her, breaking her line of sight to the man. She'd seen enough. She'd seen his darkness, his urgency, almost desperation to get to her. He'd seen her face, her mind.

10

S ammy was up in Jay's face before she'd even closed the front door behind her. 'Where have you been? Mum's going mental.'

'I needed to get out.'

'Well, thanks for leaving me...'

Jay interrupted her brother by pulling him into a hug. His body stiff at first, he relaxed and put his arms around Jay, returning her embrace. 'Sorry,' she said.

They pulled apart, and Sammy let out a sigh. He nodded towards the back room. 'She really has lost it.'

'Like, banging her head on a wall lost it, or gun in the mouth?'

Sammy shrugged. His chest fell. 'More a gentle rocking and incoherent blabbering.'

A shout came out from the lounge. 'Sammy? Is that Jay?'

Jay nodded towards the stairs. 'Can't deal with her right now, you coming?'

Sammy nodded. 'Give me a minute, I'll come up.'

Sammy headed back to the lounge as Jay crept up the stairs. Now more than ever she understood the danger she could be in, and the danger that those around her might be in for being near her. Her power was changing, bubbling below the surface, pushing to be released.

Up on the roof, Jay leaned back against the tiles and took a deep breath of the air flowing over the house from the Downs. She checked over her shoulder into her room then looked again at her wrist. The figure eight was clear.

To the north, the hills slumbered in the warmth of early afternoon while the bristling sea whispered, scratched and scraped for attention. Jay steadied her breathing, relaxing into the natural rhythm of the waves of energy as they washed over her.

The house was positioned at the boundary where the rhythmic low frequency from the hills met the spiky high energy from the sea, each leaving its mark. Jay connected. It wasn't like the colours people projected as their thoughts coalesced, and not like the words that came from those swirling colours. This was different, a mutual connection, more like a joining within the light. For a moment, Jay was part of it, and it a part of her.

'Hey.' Sammy's voice.

Jay snapped back to herself. 'What is it?' She held her fingers to her temples as if to stop her head spinning. 'Where are we?'

'On the roof. You scared me,' said Sammy, sliding down to sit on the tiles next to his sister. 'You were out of it, I couldn't wake you. It was like you were asleep with your eyes open. Weird. If you go mental like *her*, I don't think I can deal with it.'

Jay looked at her brother but said nothing, wondering if, like her, he could see the colours and hear the thoughts of others.

'You were zoned out. Were you reading someone?'

Jay frowned. 'No, that was something else. I'm still working that one out.' She sensed a disappointment in Sammy. 'Have you not felt anything yourself?' she said.

Sammy shook his head. 'I'm as normal as they come,' he said. Jay said nothing but studied her brother's profile as he looked up at the hills. She reckoned that normal would be pretty desirable right now.

en rubbed his wrist as if trying to erase the artless black marking as he looked out over the prison yard.

Scanners checked every visitor. He'd been just two weeks inside, and had twice written to Jay and Sammy, telling them to stay away. He slumped down on the concrete step next to Matchstick, his ally, who put a hand on Ben's shoulder, the black number three visible on his wrist. 'We need to get out of here,' Matchstick said.

'Not too loud,' Ben said.

'They can't read me,' said Matchstick. 'Most of the Scanners in here are weak.'

'They seem to read me well enough,' said Ben.

'You've spent too long pushing your powers away. You need to focus.'

'So how do we get out of here?'

'It's not the getting out that's the hard bit. It's staying out. As soon as you're out there, higher level Readers will be on you before you can buy your first pint.'

Ben looked at the floor, picturing that pint, sat in the pub garden at the Black Rabbit by the river. He thought of the Interland. 'What if I knew somewhere we could go? Somewhere they wouldn't be able to get to us?'

Matchstick looked at Ben, trying to read him. 'You're serious?'

Ben had been just a teenager when a Runner's touch transported him on a journey, by river, to the Interland. A safe place. The images, as real to him as if he were there, had lodged into his consciousness over the years. He could smell the rapeseed in the air, the water, the chalk. It was those images that Ben had used to craft his bedtime stories for Jay and Sammy. It was a way for him to get them out from deep inside his mind, to make them real. Unforgettable.

'I need to get out of here. We haven't much time.'

'We have nothing but time.' Matchstick raised his hands to motion around himself.

'If they take us through to rehab, there's no way back.' He locked eyes with Matchstick, daring him to contradict him. He relaxed. 'And I'm worried about Jay, I've been feeling something.'

'What?'

'She's getting stronger.'

'You can feel her from here?'

Ben nodded. 'About a hundred miles away,' he said, pride creeping into his voice.

'Shit. That's strong. You know what that means?'

Ben nodded. 'Of course. That's why we don't have much time. We have to go.'

'If you can get us somewhere safe, before they pick us up, then... yes, I can get us out of here.'

'Leave the safe place to me,' Ben said. His friend put a finger to his lips and nodded towards a guard making his

way over to them. Ben stood as the guard reached the
concrete steps.

'MacFarlane?'

Ben nodded.

'Visitor.'

* * *

JAY DIDN'T NEED the directions she'd noted down to get to
the prison from the bus station, she just headed towards the
great towers of its castle-like entrance that dominated the
skyline.

Earlier that morning, Jay had woken to the sound of
birds outside her window. She turned over in bed and
watched as a starling skipped along the ridge-tiles of the
house next door. It paused for a moment, looking in her
direction, then took off into the tree above. Jay stepped out
of bed. She needed to see her dad, whether he liked it
or not.

Turning the last corner, she looked up at the prison
through its perimeter fence topped with razor-wire. The
yellow brick building seemed to go on forever, floor upon
floor with countless rows of barred windows. A window for
each little cell, and one of those little cells for her dad. The
prison receptionist had given her strict instructions: no
scarves, no big jewellery, no sandals, no flip-flops.

After signing in, Jay was directed to a waiting area, like a
doctor's surgery with a few added extras: a vending machine
with chocolate and drinks, another with sandwiches. She
emptied her pockets into one of the lockers for visitors'
belongings and took a seat. A dog scampered into the
waiting area, a spaniel, sweeping through like a hoover with
its nose just above the floor. Its harness displayed the prison

logo in dark blue with white lettering, and a name: *Sally*. She reached Jay and sniffed at her shoes. Jay's heart raced. She calmed herself with a deep breath. Sally looked up into Jay's face for a moment, and then moved on.

A single chime of a bell signalled the visiting area was ready. Everyone filed into a room with bare, white walls. Jay's dad sat at a table in the middle of the room, sporting a patchy looking beard. He was wringing his hands.

'Hey, Dad.'

Ben stood. 'Jay.'

'Are we allowed to hug?' said Jay.

He opened his arms and held her tight.

'Stand clear!' came a shout from a guard.

As Ben released, he raised a hand to his forehead as if taking his own temperature. 'So good to see you,' he said, 'but you shouldn't have come. Shield, Jay. Please. There are people here that scan. There will be a Reader here some-where.' He looked around the room, as if trying to identify which of the guards was a Reader.

They sat down and Ben took a deep breath.

'I went to see Alf,' said Jay. Ben frowned and was about to speak when Jay continued, 'He has a map.'

'What kind of map?'

'It has the bows and arrows you told me about. But it's old, and it could be anywhere.'

'Listen to me, Jay.' Ben lowered his voice. 'Your power is strong, I can feel it. You must be a higher level than I thought.'

Jay checked in the direction of the guards and then, back to her dad, she pulled back her sleeve.

Ben stopped mid-sentence. He thrust his hand to cover her wrist, looking around the room for signs that anyone might have seen.

'Shield,' said Ben. 'You need to get away.' He looked around the room. 'Quickly, pay attention.' He opened up to her for long enough to show her his plan of escape.

Jay read the Interland on his mind; his thoughts sent anxiety flowing through her veins. The thought that her home was so unsafe that she'd have to leave too in the hope of finding truth in a myth scared her more than the idea of the Readers. Ben sensed her fear. 'Try and stay calm. I won't be in this section forever before they take me over to *education*, then *rehabilitation* – and the *Sub Levels*. The Interland could be the place where we can breathe again.'

'I'm afraid,' said Jay.

'I know. Find my notebook,' he said.

'What notebook?'

'Black cover, the one I had in the kitchen. You know the one?' Jay nodded. 'Find it and use it to figure out how to get to the gateway. There are notes in there that I have collected. Then use what *you* know.'

'I don't know anything,' Jay said.

Ben shook his head, 'You know more than anyone. It might need some piecing together.'

'This is crazy.' Jay felt a deep sadness run through her, the sense of an ending. Ben looked up and Jay followed his eyes towards the Guard. The Guard, a Reader, focused on the two of them. A chime sounded, visiting time was over. Inmates were to move to the back of the room and visitors to the front.

'Go now. Today. As soon as you get back. And take Sammy. Tell Sammy to take that little fishing book I bought for him. Don't hang about. I'll know when you've gone, I'll feel it. I have a plan.'

'You know where the Interland is?' said Jay.

He shook his head. 'I'm relying on you for that. You need

to work it out. When you figure it out, I'll know, then I'll not be far behind. Just remember the stories.'

'Seriously?'

'Find the notebook,' Ben whispered, stepping backwards towards the wall of the visiting room. Jay merged into the stream of visitors as people shuffled from the room.

In the lobby, she collected her belongings from the locker. The Reader had joined two of the security personnel. To get to the exit, Jay would have to walk directly past. She stuffed her coins and watch into her pocket as she walked, not taking her eyes off the Reader. As she reached the exit, the Reader snapped his head up and looked directly at her. She'd been seen.

The Reader pushed across the room. Jay got to the door, but the Reader caught her by the arm, spinning her around. They locked eyes. He rocked back on his heels but tightened his grip like he'd grasped an electric cable and was unable to let go. Jay's fear turned to determination. She pulled herself free, passed through the security gate and on to the exit.

Halfway across the carpark, Jay didn't need to look over her shoulder to know she was clear. She darted around the corner, and made sure her shield was up before dissolving into the maze of side streets.

12

J ay rose early, tiptoed onto the landing and leaned over the banister to see into the old crow's room on the first floor. The door was open, Mum had probably slept on the sofa and not made it to bed. She focused on the notebook then she crept down the stairs, the carpet soft under her bare feet.

Her mum's room was empty, the curtains still open from the day before. She hurried to her dad's side of the bed and riffled through his bedside cupboard. Nothing but junk, trinkets and papers. She knelt to see under the bed. Dust, cobwebs, bags of old clothes, a cardboard box. She pulled the box clear of the bed, opened it, and picked out her father's worn black notebook. Dust diffused into the air as she flicked through the pages. It was full of handwritten notes, sketches and pencil drawings. It smelled of him, of the joy he took in his writing and sketching. She smiled, losing herself for a moment as she browsed through her dad's doodles – his thoughts and feelings.

'Jay?'

Jay started. She slid the box back under the bed and made her way from her mum's room.

Sonia appeared on the landing as Jay stepped onto the stairs to the loft. 'What are you doing?' Sonia asked, her tone less confrontational than Jay was used to.

She turned, keeping the notebook concealed behind her back. 'Hey, Mum.'

Sonia leaned up against the wall and studied Jay. 'You saw him then?' Jay nodded. 'How was he?'

Jay sat on the stair, lodging the notebook behind her. 'He was OK.'

Sonia lowered her head. 'He brought it on himself, you know? Messing around with the resistance. What was he expecting to achieve? I just thank the Lord that you kids don't have to hide and lie like he has.'

Jay edged her sleeve down, making sure her wrist was covered. 'It's not his fault. It's not like he's done anything illegal. He never asked to have power.'

'Power?' Sonia croaked a laugh. 'He never had any power.' She shook her head, her eyes distant. 'Power brings influence. Your dad couldn't influence...' Jay stood. 'Wait,' said her mum. 'I'm sorry. I'm angry with him. What are we supposed to do now?'

'You could get work?' Jay turned to head up the stairs, ending the conversation. She clutched the notebook to her chest. Her west-facing bedroom was cool and dingy in the morning's shade. The walls closed in on her, squeezing the air from her lungs.

Concealing the notebook in her backpack, Jay crept down to the first floor landing. She made sure there was no sign of her mum then poked her head around Sammy's door. Light snoring radiated from under his duvet. She sat on the edge of his bed and peeled back the covers. 'Hey,' she whispered. Sammy jerked awake, wide-eyed, then settled back down, grumbled and closed his eyes again.

She flicked his ear, and he pulled away. 'What? Go away.'

'I found Dad's notebook.'

Sammy turned over and squinted at her. 'You found it? Already?'

'Under Mum's bed. I won't read it here, I'm heading out.'

'You want me to come?'

'No, you sleep,' Jay said, but she needn't have bothered. Sammy's eyes were already closed.

* * *

JAY HEADED to the disused pier. Under the old timbers of the deck, she ducked below the safety fence that kept the tourists out, and sat on the stones where she could lean back on one of the wooden deck supports. On the post in front of her she could see her a carving of her name, faded over the years since she'd scratched it into the wood with a piece of flint. Stitch's name was there too, but not Cassie's. Their friendship with Cassie had come later.

The sound of the sea was hypnotic – the crash of the waves breaking over the sand then the suck and sweep as the sea pulled back the pebbles. Sandflies buzzed around the drying seaweed wrapped to the pier's wooden posts. Jay settled herself into the stones, opened the notebook and started at the beginning.

* * *

HER DAD'S notes were simple in places, cryptic in others. His pencil drawings were intricate. The images drifted through her mind as she walked from the beach to the bookshop on the corner, choosing the longer route along the seafront.

The visit to the prison and her time spent with his notebook reminded Jay of their shared sense of adventure, the excitement they had in solving a puzzle, the connection between minds they'd once made when she was little. She felt a pang of longing. What she wouldn't give to have him here, solving this impossible puzzle with her. She needed help.

The bell rang above Alf's door. A woman Jay had never seen sat behind the bookshop's desk. He was always there, never anyone but him. 'Where's Alf?'

'Who?' the woman said.

'Alfred, the bookseller. It's his shop.'

'If you mean the previous *manager*, he's moved on.' The woman returned her attention to the papers on the checkout and Jay sensed her power. The scrawny, gripey woman was attempting to read Jay so she put up her shield. Her heart thumped. The woman's power was weak. She wouldn't be able to read Jay, but she might sense her power.

Jay stepped back, turned and headed for the stairs, continuing to shield. At the foot of the stairs, she slowed, refocused. She saw that Alf had been taken for questioning by the Readers. In the woman's mind, she saw the Reader, a tall man with a scar from temple to chin. The Reader was strong, Alfred no match for him. Jay stopped, attempting to get her breath.

'Can I help you?' the woman asked.

Jay shook her head and climbed the stairs. She'd been exposed for sure. The woman at the desk would bring the Readers in for Jay. She picked up speed, taking the stairs two at a time, knowing she ought to head in the opposite direction – away from the shop.

The top floor had been closed off with strips of yellow warning tape. A handwritten sign said 'closed for maintenance'. Jay ducked under the barricade. The top stair gave a familiar creak. She made her way to the shelves at the back.

Someone had removed all literature on the Given. The entire bottom shelf had been cleared, along with sections of the next two shelves up. Jay's heart raced as she searched for the Sasha Colden book. Nothing. Everything was gone.

Her fear rising, Jay moved quickly. She jumped up and covered the distance to the cabinet by the stairs in two strides. It was locked, but the lock was flimsy and three hard pulls burst it open. The lock breaking sounded like a gunshot in the quiet store and now Jay knew she was in deep. Inside the cabinet, the Colden book stared back at her. She slid it into her backpack and turned towards the stairs.

A wave of energy buffeted her. A Reader was close. She backtracked, ducking behind a set of shelves. Two men in black clothes emerged from the stairs. Jay stood rooted to the floor as the men poured into the room, their energy expanding into every corner. They separated, circling the room and blocking both exits. Jay's skin prickled with fear. She shielded, considering making a run for the stairs. The taller of the two men slowed and turned towards Jay as if sensing her. She couldn't see his face. He turned again and continued.

After a circuit the two men regrouped, leaving Jay a glimpse of a path to the back exit. She stumbled out from the cover of the shelves of books and sensed them turn. She felt the tall one spy her and a piercing blackness burrowed into her.

Jay pushed through the fire escape door and onto the stairs, launching herself down the steps, losing her footing in her desperation to flee. She half-ran, half-fell to ground level before the fire escape door above opened. Jay looked up, frozen. The men began their descent, taking their time, unhurried. Jay could see the scar on the tall man's face from two floors down. Her legs trembled. Terror spread through her body. As the men reached the first floor, adrenaline pumped life into her body and Jay turned and ran.

13

J ay got home as the sun dipped behind the hill. She slammed the front door then leaned against it, steadying her breath. She was glad to put a barrier between her and the Readers even if it wasn't likely to stop them.

With no sign of Sammy or her mum, she made straight for her room. She paused at the top of the stairs, hearing music.

At the sound of the door opening, Cassie glanced up from flipping through records, her tight beaded braids swishing back and forth. Stitch jumped, threw his cigarette out of the window and held his breath. He coughed, relieved to see Jay. 'Thought you were the old crow.' He gathered himself and scrambled up to lean out of the window and pick his half-smoked cigarette from the roof tiles. 'Where have you been?'

'Beach,' she said, standing in the middle of the room. 'Then the bookshop.'

Cassie looked up from the stack of records. 'Sammy's out there,' she said, nodding towards the window.

Jay climbed out to sit on the roof with her brother who was looking out over the hills towards the sunset on the horizon. 'Hey. Did you read the notebook?'

Jay nodded. 'Yep.'

'What do you reckon then?'

'Bumped into a couple of Readers in the bookshop. And Alf's gone.'

Sammy's mouth dropped open.

'They clocked me, but I gave them the slip.'

'Wha...' Sammy stuttered, 'did they sense you? Were they looking for you?'

'Maybe. The top floor was cordoned off and a lot of the old books were gone. They came up looking for me.'

'They won't follow you here?'

Cassie and Stitch joined them on the roof, looking at Jay with concern as she answered her brother, 'No. I don't think so,' Jay said, pulling her dad's notebook and the Sasha Colden biography from her bag. As well as her own bookmark poking out, there were other papers crammed into the back of the book. Jay opened it and pulled out the old map that she and Alf had been looking at. Sammy watched as Jay unfolded it, revealing the drawing of the bows and arrows. At the top of the map was a post-it note with handwriting that Jay recognised. 'This is from Alf.'

Sammy read it aloud: *Leave. It's not safe.* He leaned back against the tiles.

'He knew I'd come for the book,' said Jay.

They looked out into the darkness, over the tops of the trees and on to the Downs. Jay could smell the salt in the breeze coming off the beach.

'I reckon we could find it, if it exists,' Jay said. She nodded towards the horizon where the moonlit grey sky touched the black that marked the tops of the trees. 'You see that light flickering over there?'

Sammy sat up straight. 'Yeah?'

'That's Highdown. You know, where we used to take the go-kart with Dad. Every night this time of year there's someone up there lighting a bonfire, summoning the spirits or some other shit.'

Stitch piped up, 'Ley lines, it's not shit.'

'I've been trying to figure something out,' said Jay. 'In the notebook, and Alf's map, the sketches...'

Cassie let out a sigh, interrupting Jay's flow for a moment. 'We've talked about this before. For *years*. If it exists, what makes you think you can find it when no one else ever has?'

Cassie's grandad had disappeared just after they moved to the area. She blamed him for his absence, couldn't talk about him. Losing her grandad came not long after losing her childhood soul mate. Stitch piped up again. 'Of course it exists. You should know, Cassie. Your grandad talked about it all the time.'

'We don't know it's the same place. And don't talk about my grandad. You don't know what he said.'

'I know what you told us.'

'Leave it, you two,' Jay intervened.

'My grandad talked about a place he called "the caverns", but he said nothing about any Interland, and he let nothing useful slip about where the caverns are. There's no reason to think it's the same place, and there's nothing to say that either place is real.'

'Except what Jay's dad said, and his notebook.'

The four of them fell silent. Jay rested her head and searched the sky for the plough, but the stars were dim in the grey-black sky. The only sound was Sammy flicking through the pages of the notebook. She looked at Cassie, then to Stitch. 'Anything?' she said, motioning to her wrist. They both shook their heads as Jay pulled back her sleeve.

She watched as Stitch's eyes widened and he slapped his hand down on the roof tiles. 'I knew it,' he said, pulling Jay's hand closer so that he could study the marking. Jay caught Sammy's eye and he smiled, giving a little nod before turning back to the notebook. Cassie's smile was more strained. She looked away, into the distance.

Sammy looked at Jay. 'This is serious. That marking settles things. We have no choice.'

'Sammy's right,' said Stitch, still holding on to Jay's wrist. 'This is big. This is, like, a magnet. It will draw the Readers in sooner or later.'

Sammy continued to turn the pages of the notebook. 'I reckon he's put enough in here for us to figure out where this place is. If anyone can understand Dad, and make the link between this stuff and his stories, then it's you, right?'

'I think the hill forts are the link,' said Jay.

'How?' said Sammy.

'You remember what Dad said about the Interland? His story about trekking downstream along the River Arun?'

Sammy shrugged. 'I remember bits of it.'

'The maps show the Arun running through the Downs to the estuary on the coast, and, according to Dad's stories, the gateway is at the intersect of ley lines bounded by the ancient hill forts. Like in that map from Alf. The Arun runs right through the Downs, through the area of three hill forts.'

'So it could be right out there?' said Stitch, motioning to the hills in the distance.

'That's one of them.' Jay pointed towards the light

winking on the horizon. 'Highdown. Then there's one at Cissbury, and one at Chanctonbury.'

Stitch looked at Jay. 'So, we follow the lines through the three hill forts and find the gateway?'

'Something like that, but they're not on a line, and there's no obvious standout confluence of rivers. There are various tributaries of the Arun that cross with the Rother and the Wey, but no obvious point within the zone of the hill forts. So, I don't know.' Jay leaned over towards her brother to point him at a page in the notebook, a sketch of what looked like a map.

'What's that?' said Stitch.

'It's the closest thing to a map that's in the whole notebook,' said Jay. 'But it doesn't tie up with Alf's map.'

Sammy looked at her. 'You know that book Dad gave me, the fishing book?'

'The engrossing *Fishing With Spinners*,' Jay smiled. 'Dad mentioned that. He wanted you to bring it.'

'You know about the drawings in the back?'

'What drawings?'

'It has a hand-drawn sketch in the back.'

'A map?'

'No. It's more of a sketch of points, like a constellation or something. I always assumed it was just one of Dad's doodles.'

'Go and get it.'

Sammy disappeared through the window, returning a minute later with the little hardback book. He flicked to the back page before handing it to Jay, who studied it.

'Enlightenment?' said Cassie.

'The link between the rivers and the hill forts. The bows and arrows. It might be something.'

Sammy studied the sketches for a minute then looked up. 'So we start there.' He pointed towards Highdown.

'How are we supposed to get there? It's more than a day's walk to Highdown from here. Got to be twenty miles.' What Jay didn't put word to were her misgivings about involving her little brother and friends in what was likely a dangerous mission.

Sammy smiled. 'We can take Dad's car. The Beast. You can drive.'

Jay shook her head, 'It hasn't moved for years,' she said.

'So? It still runs,' said Sammy. 'I started it the other day.'

'I'm in,' said Stitch. 'Let's do it. We can chuck a couple of the tents in the boot. How long till we get to the gateway?'

'Depends where it is, Stitch. We don't know yet,' Jay said.

Sammy thought for a moment then said, 'If we drive, we can get to the car park at the foot of Highdown and trek up to the summit. Maybe a couple of hours. Then we see how we go from there. We should plan to be sleeping under the stars for a few nights at least.'

'Or in the car,' said Cassie.

Stitch shook his head. 'No way I'm sleeping in a car. Tried that. Worst night's sleep ever.'

'Let's not go mad,' said Jay, 'let's think about this. We can't just up and go chasing...'

'Dad needs us to go. He said so,' said Sammy.

'What if he's wrong?' said Jay.

Sammy and Stitch looked at Jay. 'What if he's right?' they said at the same time.

14

L ong after Stitch and Cassie had gone home, Jay and Sammy stayed on the roof, making plans. Stitch was going home to pack his rucksack. Cassie was non-committal but Stitch insisted she be ready in the morning.

Jay sighed, worried for Sammy, anxious that as soon as they left home, came out in the open, the Readers would track them. It was one thing shielding within the safety of home, behind brick walls, but out in the open it was more difficult. Her energy would be easier for Readers to detect.

'Is Dad out yet?' asked Sammy.

'I don't know.'

'Can't you look?'

'Where Dad is concerned I have a block. I can't seem to get through to him from a distance.'

'I thought he said he could hear you, sense you?'

'But I can't hear him. I don't know why.'

Sammy yawned. 'Look, Jay, get some sleep. We leave early.' Sammy smiled and disappeared through the window.

Jay looked at her watch: almost 1 am. She reached in

through her window and plucked the hipflask of her dad's whiskey from the drawer in her bedside table. She'd lifted it from her dad's coat after he was taken. She unscrewed the cap and sniffed at the top, the smell reminding her of him. She took a swig and winced at the taste, then coughed as it hit her chest. It warmed her. She forced another swig and the night chill didn't feel so harsh. She lay back against the tiles. The flickering light up at Highdown had disappeared. She turned on her side, looked out towards the sea and closed her eyes.

All was quiet at first. Nothing but a gentle ebb and flow of whispers from the depths. 'Tell me what to do,' Jay said into the night. The noise grew as Jay attuned, the whispers becoming a consistent white-noise. She sifted the sounds, filtered, collected and grouped them. But the noise was so desperate, chaotic. 'Slow down,' Jay said aloud, feeling as though she were being cajoled into something. 'What is it?' she whispered back to the sea, and the sounds seemed to sink back into the wind and the waves, allowing Jay to drift off to sleep.

* * *

SHE WOKE SENSING A PRESENCE, shivering in the cold coming from the roof tiles, and pulled herself into a tight ball.

A noise. She strained to hear, then lifted her head to see through the window into her room. Nothing. She struggled for her eyes to adjust to the darkness inside. 'Is someone there?' she said.

The figure of a man emerged from the shadows and into the light of the half-moon, scruffily dressed in dark clothes. In a short-sleeved shirt he made no attempt to hide the mark on his wrist, labelling him as a level six. Jay opened her mouth but no sound came. Before she could move, the man reached and dragged Jay by her top and her hair, back through the window. She closed her eyes with the pain and screamed aloud. The man clamped his hand over her mouth and Jay silently screamed Stitch's name into her head. He threw her down on her bed and pulled back his fist before putting a finger to his lips.

'Who's Stitch?' the man asked.

Jay's breathing was shallow and rapid, her hands shaking. She told herself to calm down. He came closer. 'You have power. Like your dad.' Jay edged back against the wall. 'I came for the notebook,' the man said, 'but what a bonus. How have we not seen you before?' Jay recoiled further as he leaned forward and pulled her sleeve. 'Level eight,' he said, leaning away from her. The man gathered himself and stared into her. 'You are something quite different.'

* * *

STITCH SAT bolt upright in bed. 'Jay!' he shouted.

He scratched his head, eyes half-closed and looking around his room as if trying to figure out where he was. 'Jay?' he said aloud.

He laid back down and pulled his duvet over his head. A bad dream. Something about Jay. A man threatening her.

'Jay!' Stitch shouted again, once more sitting bolt upright. He checked his watch: 3 am. He flung himself out of bed and scrabbled around for the clothes he'd dumped on the floor.

He grabbed his rucksack, packed the night before, his tent strapped to its base. He made his way downstairs, bumping and scraping with his rucksack against the wall, pictures knocked squint, not bothering to be quiet – it would take an earthquake before his dad would even stir. Reaching the telephone in the hallway, Stitch punched in 999 and waited for the emergency services operator.

'Police, please.'

The voice on the other end was slow and calm, insisting on Stitch giving his name and location before she would listen to the nature of the emergency. Stitch relayed the details of Jay's situation, that there was an intruder in her house, skipping the bit about how Jay had contacted him. The operator dispatched a response team to Jay's address and asked him to stay on the line. Stitch hung up and dialled the number for Cassie's house.

Cassie's brother Charlie answered the phone. 'Hello?'

'Charlie, it's Stitch. Get Cassie for me, it's urgent.'

'She's asleep, Stitch.'

'How weird,' Stitch said. 'I know she's asleep, it's 3 am. Please get her, Charlie, tell her to hurry.'

A long minute passed before Cassie came on the line. 'What's up?'

'It's Jay. She's in trouble. I've called the police and they're on their way round there. We need to go.'

'Go where?'

'To Jay's, meet me in the car park at the One Stop outside your place. Two minutes.' Stitch hung up the phone before Cassie could argue. He took one last look back into his house, the sound of his dad's snoring echoing down the stairs, before turning and leaving by the front door.

* * *

CASSIE WAS ALREADY in the car park as Stitch emerged from the alleyway and into the light of the streetlamps.

'You were quick,' said Stitch.

'You said two minutes,' said Cassie, her arms hugging herself for warmth. 'It's been nearly three minutes.'

They set off towards Jay's house. 'Where's your stuff?' said Stitch.

'What stuff?'

'In case we need to hit the road.'

'I'm sorry, what...?'

'Cassie, come on...'

'Stitch!' Cassie stopped dead.

'OK, walk and I'll talk.' Stitch filled Cassie in on the message he'd heard from Jay. It then took all of Stitch's persuasive powers to stop Cassie turning around and going straight home. Then they saw two men standing outside Jay's house.

'Get back!' Stitch pulled Cassie back into the darkness of the bushes before she could step out into the lamplight.

'Who is it?'

'I don't know, but they don't look like police.' As Stitch said this, a police car emerged, crawling around the corner without its blue lights flashing. It pulled up outside Jay's house.

'They're in no hurry,' said Cassie. Two officers emerged from the vehicle and approached the men. They shook hands. 'Those guys must be Scanners.'

'Readers,' corrected Cassie, edging back further. 'This isn't good.'

After a few moments, the uniformed officers returned to their car.

'We need to get in there,' said Stitch. 'If they figure out who Jay is, they'll take her away. She won't stand a chance.'

'And we will?' said Cassie.

'We can try. Round the back.' Stitch took off running,

bent over double, around the houses to the back of Jay's garden. Cassie followed.

Stitch dropped his rucksack at the foot of the tree and they shinned up and onto the roof. Stitch peeked in through the open Velux. Jay was on the floor, face down and motionless. A dark shadow of a man rooted through the drawers beneath her desk. As Stitch watched, he emptied each drawer onto the floor and sifted through the debris with gloved hands. Stitch and Cassie looked at each other, unsure what to do.

Jay's bedroom door opened. Sammy walked in and stopped when he saw his sister lying prone on the floor. Before Stitch or Cassie could call a warning, the man stepped from the shadows and held a cloth to Sammy's face. Sammy struggled, but not for long. After he'd been laid face down beside his sister, the man resumed his chaotic searching.

Cassie pressed her mouth against Stitch's ear and whispered, 'I'll create a diversion. You get them out.'

Before Stitch could answer, Cassie stood and threw open the window with a single, purposeful move and shouted, 'Come on Jay,' in a slurred voice. 'Come out and play.'

Cassie wobbled and teetered on the roof, walking the ridge tiles. The man came to the window and watched her for a moment before pulling himself out onto the roof. 'You should get down from there,' he said.

Cassie stopped and made as if she were squinting to see who he was. 'Well,' she slurred, 'she never told me she had a fancy man.'

'No? Well, I'm offended.'

Cassie wobbled. 'I'm just surprised,' she said, then faked a hiccup.

'Surprised?'

'She would never normally go for someone like...'

'Like what?' the man said, looking around for his best route up the roof slope to get to Cassie.

'Like, short and a little soft around the middle,' Cassie laughed and then made as if she'd tripped, scuttling down the slope of the roof towards the man. He caught her, and they spun around, leaving Stitch a clear path to climb unseen through the window.

Inside, Sammy had woken and was bent over Jay, trying to wake her.

'What's going on?' Sammy asked.

'Readers, we need to go, like right now. There are two more outside.'

'They've come for me,' Jay croaked.

Stitch said to Sammy, 'Grab your stuff. We're leaving now. Be quick!' Sammy ducked out of the room.

Noises from the roof told Stitch that Cassie's drunken charade continued. 'Jay, can you get up? We need to go.' Jay nodded and struggled to her feet. Stitch helped as Jay threw some bits into her bag – the notebook from under her mattress, along with Sammy's fishing book. Spare clothes. A sleeping bag and torch. Sammy arrived back in the room, a rucksack on his back. He nodded at Stitch and the three of them turned to the window.

Cassie had collapsed against the Reader, forcing him to hold her up as they teetered near the edge of the roof. Their backs were turned. Stitch climbed out of the window first, followed by Sammy. As Jay's feet met the tiles, the Reader pushed Cassie aside and turned. He brought his fingers up to his temple. Jay said, 'The others are coming.'

Cassie took her opportunity, brought her shoulder down and, taking him by surprise, sent the Reader over the edge of the roof and into the neighbouring garden.

They peered over the edge at the man tangled in the hedgerow. 'We need to go right now,' Jay said, then glanced back at her room.

Stitch followed her gaze. He could hear that the other two Readers had arrived.

Sammy slammed the Velux window closed. 'Let's go.'

The four of them scrambled down the tree. Stitch hiked his rucksack onto his back and lurched into the alleyway that led to the lockup, where the car was parked. Sammy opened the up-and-over garage door and threw the keys to Jay. She climbed into the front seat of the old Ford and froze.

'What is it?' said Stitch from the back seat.

'Smells of Dad, that manky Drum rolling tobacco he used to smoke.'

'Can we reminisce later maybe?' said Stitch.

Sammy put a hand on her shoulder. 'We really need to move.' Jay turned the key in the ignition. The starter motor whirred and turned over, but the engine didn't fire. Sammy screamed. Two men had turned the corner of the garage. Jay fumbled for the keys in the ignition. Stitch and Cassie joined Sammy in screaming for Jay to move. On the second try the Beast did not disappoint. It sparked into life, rumbling and spluttering. Jay released the clutch and stamped on the accelerator. The car slammed both men into the sides of the garage as it squeezed past at speed, swept away through the gravel car park and into the warren of back streets.

PART III

INTO THE WOODS

15

Cassie had insisted on picking up a few supplies before they headed into the middle of nowhere and as far as Stitch could tell she had no sense of urgency. While they waited, Sammy fiddled with the dial on the car's radio, receiving little but static. Sammy would never see fault in anything that Cassie did. He'd wait a year if that's what she asked of him.

Only Jay seemed to know how much danger they were in. She could feel the Readers.

They were coming.

The streetlamp next to the car flickered and died and Stitch wondered if it was a sign. The rest of the lights in the street blinked out one by one, taking the orange sheen off the morning and revealing its grey reality.

Stitch turned to Jay. 'Did you say anything to your mum about leaving?'

'No time.'

'I wrote my dad a note last night,' said Stitch. ' A long note. More of an essay, actually.'

'Seriously?'

'If he won't talk to me...'

'What did you say?'

'Everything. Laid it all out there.'

'Did it help?' asked Jay.

'I think so. I guess we'll see when all this is over.' He turned to the window. 'Finally,' he said, as Cassie appeared from the alleyway, rucksack on her back. He looked up at Jay, willing her to start the engine, put the beast into gear and hold the clutch. Sammy turned and watched, a weak smile on his face as Cassie sauntered towards the car.

'Oh, seriously, *come on*,' said Stitch.

'Ready?' said Jay, as Cassie closed the boot and climbed in next to Stitch.

'I guess,' said Cassie.

'What did you say to your parents?' Sammy asked.

Cassie shrugged. 'They won't notice I'm gone.' Stitch knew that Cassie was exaggerating her parents' disinterest. Her brother might not register her absence, but her parents would flip.

'But you left them a note or something?' said Jay.

Cassie nodded. 'Said we were going camping.'

* * *

JAY PULLED the old Ford into the car park. They had a steady hour or so climb ahead of them, then through the valley and up to the ring of trees at the Highdown summit.

Stitch opened the boot. Sammy pulled his rucksack from the car. 'It'll be warm tonight. Perfect for a night under the stars.' They tightened the straps of their rucksacks and headed into the trees.

Under the cover of trees, Stitch relaxed a little, feeling at last hidden from the Readers who would be sure to be tracking them. He glanced at Jay. He sensed her worry for her little brother and best friends, her guilt at dragging them all into danger. She would have to dig deep to develop her strength, her power, but she still seemed reluctant to let go and embrace it.

The four stayed close to the edge of the woods, wading through bracken out of sight of the road. Jay led the way to higher ground, navigating on instinct. Within an hour, they had made it onto the chalk ridge and stepped out from the trees. The countryside opened up in widescreen, the sun now directly overhead.

Chest-high rapeseed ran away down the vast slope, thickening to a homogenous sunflower yellow at the bottom of the valley. To the northwest, nearer now, was Highdown.

'Let's rest. Up there.' Jay motioned to a high point on the chalk ridge.

They sat on the hard ground and ate biscuits. Sammy fashioned a small fire to test out his camping kettle, excited when they heard the whistle. Stitch noticed Jay rubbing her temples. 'What happened back there?' Jay said, almost to herself.

'I'm guessing he used some kind of tranquilizer, maybe ether,' said Stitch. 'You were out when we got there.' He looked over at Sammy, 'Hey, Sammy, how's the head?'

Sammy rubbed his forehead. 'Still throbbing.'

'Impressive performance from Cassie though,' said Stitch.

She smiled. 'Enjoyed seeing him plant head first into a hedge.'

Jay looked up into the distance. 'I don't think that will be the last we see of them.'

Stitch gazed over the patchwork landscape. The hill at Highdown was clear, a few miles west of their location. To the northeast was the ring of trees at Cissbury, another high point on the chalk Downs. Like Highdown, Cissbury was a hilltop peppered with trees and falling steeply on all sides. Perfect for sledging in winter. From the top you can see past Brighton to the chalk cliffs in the east, and back towards Highdown. Chanctonbury was out of sight, four or five miles to the north. From above, the three hill forts formed a triangle with each side between five and ten miles long.

'See Cissbury Ring,' Stitch said, pointing.

'Listen a minute.' Jay raised her left arm in the direction of Highdown and her right towards Cissbury. 'The connection of the three hill forts makes a triangle. Like a bow. Imagine it with an arrow pointing towards a fourth location.'

'To the gateway?'

'Maybe, but I don't know which direction the arrow points. I'm hoping we will see when we get to Highdown. But even if we do, there must be another line, a trajectory that intersects this one.'

'How do we find the second line?' said Stitch.

'I'm hoping for divine inspiration,' she said. 'We need to get up to Highdown.'

16

S titch led the way into the valley. The four of them strung out as they crossed a wooden bridge over a stream, then over a stile and back into the trees before beginning the climb. The shade of the trees brought relief from the glare and heat of the sun. Stitch rested a moment to allow the group to collect before pressing on.

Stitch knew Highdown Hill as well as Jay did. When Jay's dad made a makeshift go-kart from an old pram, they spent Sunday afternoons racing and rattling down the steep chalk slopes. Its wheels were the size of a car's wheels, with thin white rubber strips for tyres. They bounced around on a chipboard base for hours, scraping through narrow gaps and over bumps and humps, screaming and laughing while narrowly avoiding injury. Stitch's arms would get covered in scratches from the hawthorn bushes, their only means of braking, his legs battered and bruised from nicks and bumps on trees and branches.

At the top of Highdown, Stitch turned full circle to look over the fields, and then across to the copse of trees at the summit. He strained his eyes to see if Chanctonbury or Cissbury were visible from where he stood but it was too dark and murky to see. The sea was invisible through the clouds but present in the salty breeze coming over the hill.

'Hey,' said Jay, interrupting Stitch from his thoughts. 'I know where we can set up camp.' She led the way towards the ring of trees at the top of the hill. When Jay entered the copse, she looked as though she'd come up against an invisible barrier. Stitch watched as she doubled back, saying nothing, and found another way to enter the trees.

'What's up?' said Stitch.

'This is the way in,' said Jay. All the hill-fort settlements had distinct entrance points, but these were no longer visible above ground, long buried under layers of history.

Jay chose a quiet spot, within the outer circle of trees but away from the main paths, the central point, and the inner circle. Stitch recognised the terrain from his time up there with Jay and her dad. On the eastern slope, the chalk outcrop dove to a trough that was difficult to negotiate if you were unfamiliar with it. 'Watch your step through there,' he said to Sammy as they side-stepped down to the lower ridge. The view to the north was vast and sheltered from the south wind.

Cassie dumped her bag and turned to Sammy. 'We're gonna need a good fire.'

'On it,' said Sammy.

'You OK?' Stitch asked.

She nodded, forcing a smile. 'They'll be tracking us.'

'You'll know if they get close,' said Stitch.

Jay sighed. 'I hope so,' she said.

'Why don't we set up camp and see if we can see Cissbury and Chanctonbury from here. There might be fires tonight.'

* * *

STITCH'S EYELIDS GREW HEAVY. Sammy flicked through his little hardback book on spin fishing as Cassie and Jay stood looking north over the ridge, Ben's notebook open in Jay's hands.

Stitch shook away his fatigue and stood to join them. 'Chanctonbury?' he said, squinting to see a flicker of orange light in the distance.

Jay nodded. 'And that's Cissbury.' She pointed towards a larger orange glow further east. 'That's the first bow-shape from the legend. The line from here to Chanctonbury is the long edge, the handle of the bow. Then from here to Cissbury, and from Cissbury to Chanctonbury, is the string of the bow, held taut at Cissbury.'

Stitch said, 'That's what you drew on your map?'

'Yes, but the thing you can't see on the map is there.' Jay pointed.

Stitch squinted. 'What?'

'See the line of trees that runs from Cissbury? Thin line of poplars. They run directly from Cissbury to that village.'

'What is it?' Sammy said, joining them.

'I get it. That's the arrow,' said Stitch. 'The trajectory.'

'Exactly. But it doesn't tell us the distance,' said Jay.

* * *

SAT BY THE FIRE, Stitch studied Jay's map, marking out the line of the trees that projected from Cissbury. He and Jay had figured the precise angles from the location of Findon Village in the distance, visible by the streetlights. From this, they marked a line on the map that extended through the

Downs, hoping that it would cross a location with a mapped confluence of rivers, but there was none.

'Nothing?' said Cassie, unable to hide her irritation.

'Nothing where two rivers meet. There are a bunch of rivers, tributaries, lakes, all sorts,' said Stitch.

'That's what I found before,' said Jay. 'We need the other trajectory so we can find the intersect.'

'Where's the other bow and bloody arrow then?' said Cassie. Stitch and Jay were silent. Sammy stood and looked out towards the glow at Cissbury.

Stitch closed his eyes and took a breath. He'd read a lot about the hill forts, and their supposed power. He believed in Jay, and her powers, and he sensed her strength growing, fuelled by the energy of the land.

'Stitch?' Jay interrupted his thoughts. 'Remind me what the legend says about the second set of lines, the second bow and arrow?'

Stitch flicked through Ben's notebook, then spoke slowly, dictating the transcription of the legend. 'From the second bow came a second arrow, in a wave of mutilation...'

'Charming,' said Sammy.

'Are there any sea-forts down on the coast?' said Cassie.

'Why?' said Sammy.

'Cassie's right. The wave,' said Jay. 'Could be the wave as in the sea.'

'Exactly,' said Cassie.

'Why *mutilation*?' said Sammy. 'I don't like the sound of that.'

The four of them crowded around Jay's map, tilting it towards the fire for light. Stitch searched the nearby coast on the map for a sign of a fort.

'What about Bamber?' said Stitch, pointing to the castle on the map.

'That's nowhere near the coast, and probably a few hundred years after the time of the legend,' said Jay.

Stitch thought hard, trying to find a link. 'Down at Beach Lane, the café there, you remember? We've been there loads.'

'The grannie café?' said Cassie.

'On the wall in there,' said Stitch. 'They have all those old pictures.'

'You actually looked at those?' said Cassie.

'They talk about Bamber Castle, which used to be on the coast, before the coast moved. Bamber was built as a fortification of existing points of defence on the coast.'

'How do you even know this stuff?' said Cassie.

'I can read,' Stitch said without looking at Cassie. He stared at Jay, willing his enthusiasm to break the surface and give him an ally.

'That's it,' said Jay. 'We need to go for a coffee and cake session.'

'What?' said Sammy.

'Beach Lane Café, we need to get down there.' Jay stood as if to head off.

'Rest first,' said Stitch. 'We have the first bow, and the trajectory. We can go at first light, head back to the car, then get there for that breakfast you wanted, Sammy.'

Jay nodded, took the notebook from Stitch, and settled by the fire. Stitch watched her turning the pages of her dad's notebook and thought of his dad, wondered if he'd be worried.

In his note, he explained how he'd felt frozen out of his dad's life since his mum's death. He looked over at Jay, the light of the fire giving her an unearthly glow. He tried to understand what it would take for his friend to delve deeper into her power, to use the inner strength that Stitch knew was there.

She turned to him and spoke. 'We need to be careful. If I open up too much, I'll end up leading those Readers straight to us, and to the gateway.'

'You need to see what those powers can do if we are to stand any chance of fending them off. We don't know how many of them there are. Or how close they are. If your power is growing like your dad said, then you are our best chance.'

Jay lowered her gaze again. Stitch watched as Jay slipped into sleep, the flicker of light from the fire dancing across her face, lighting the curve of her cheek and accentuating her lips.

17

Stitch couldn't sleep. Sammy and Cassie huddled for warmth, both asleep. Jay had turned over and was facing away from him, her shoulder rising and falling with her steady breathing. The fire was reduced to embers, but up in the trees behind them an intermittent orange glow flickered. He pulled up the hood of his jacket and climbed to the edge of the inner circle.

Around a small fire in the middle of the clearing were six or seven figures sat on logs. Stitch watched from behind a tree. Outside their circle of log seats they had candles on spikes, embedded in the ground. He caught the occasional scent of incense.

Stitch had read about the pagan rituals up at the hill forts on the Downs. As he watched, one of the figures rose and walked around the circle of candles and back to his seat, like a child's game. There was no music, no rhythmic drumming, no chanting. It was peaceful. He counted the revolutions made by the next figure. 'Six,' he said aloud.

'Seven.' A voice from behind him.

Stitch jumped. An adrenaline spike fizzed across his

skin. He turned to see a tall man, caped and hooded like Obi-Wan. 'Seven,' the man repeated. 'Those in the inner circle each make seven revolutions in the time it takes the seventh member, me, to make seven revolutions of this circle.' He nodded at the tree that Stitch leaned against, a tree that formed part of the inner circle.

'You scared me,' Stitch said, his heart still pounding.

'Join us if you like? Where are your friends?'

'Asleep,' Stitch said.

'Come,' the man said, heading around the circle for a distance before turning in to cross the treeline. Despite himself, Stitch stepped forward. 'No,' the man said, clear and firm. 'Here, come through here.' He pointed between two trees.

The figures watched as they approached. Obi-Wan pointed to a log for Stitch. They each pushed down their hoods so that Stitch could see their faces. Of the seven, three were women. All were middle-aged, all were smiling like they were happy for the new company.

'Why seven?' said Stitch.

Obi-Wan introduced himself then. 'Dave. I'm from London.'

'My friends call me Stitch.'

The others did the same and Stitch took in some of their names – Sally, Joe... all from London.

'Why seven revolutions?' Stitch repeated.

The woman named Sally spoke. 'It's a protection ritual,' she smiled. 'We put back what those of ignorance have opened up. One of the myths says that if you complete seven circuits of the inner circle of trees in the time it takes for the clock to strike twelve times, then the devil will appear. So people try it. They don't realise they're unwinding the coils. The Devil won't appear of course, but they inflict damage, nonetheless. So we come and make the necessary repairs. Seven inner circuits by seven people in the time it takes for seven circuits of the outer circle of trees. Once a month is enough.'

'Wow,' said Stitch.

'You think we're crazy, don't you,' another of the figures said, passing a bottle around for Stitch.

'No thanks.' Stitch waved away the bottle, thinking of the blood-drinking scene in the *Lost Boys*. 'So are you done for the month? Was that it, Devil's access route all closed up?'

They laughed and another bottle of wine was retrieved from a bag. The man next to Sally whispered something in her ear and she looked over, catching Stitch's eye for a moment before he had to look away.

'Joe thinks you have power,' she said.

Stitch looked at Joe and back to Sally, shaking his head. Joe spoke. 'Not in the traditional sense, I don't think.' He looked towards Stitch's wrist. 'I think you have something a little different.' Stitch remained speechless, with a strong sense that he should get away before it was too late, but at the same time a curiosity that glued his feet to the floor. Joe continued. 'Do you have a marking?'

Stitch pulled up his sleeve to show nothing but a pale wrist. Joe stood, examining his wrist and then taking a seat next to him. 'I'm getting a sense of a power in you.'

Stitch smiled and leaned away from Joe. 'Well, that's where you're wrong, my friend.'

'Do you know anything about spiritual healing?'

Stitch shrugged, looking at Joe. 'It's all about the transfer of energy,' Joe said. 'It's not religious.'

Stitch glanced at Sally for reassurance. She smiled back at him and then shook her head. 'Joe, leave him be.'

Joe continued to look at Stitch as if he were peering *into* him. 'It's more about the promotion of natural self-healing by bringing a state of balance, connecting things.'

'Why are you telling me this?'

Joe laughed, then stood to return to his seat. 'I'm saying that you have something of the healer in you. Like me. You bring the energy together, connect it. I bet you're a middle child?'

Stitch shook his head. 'Only child,' he said. He sat and talked with them for some time, sharing in their stories. As he began to yawn more frequently, thinking about getting back before he passed the point of sleep, the pagans rose one by one to leave. 'You're not driving back to London now?' Stitch said, thinking of the volume of wine that they all seemed to have drunk.

'Dave's driving. Tee-total. And he has a minibus licence.' They laughed and began to file towards the south edge of the circle.

'Good to meet you. Good luck on your journey.'

Joe hung back a moment, reached into his bag and pulled out a book, handing it to Stitch. 'You have this. I can get hold of another copy,' he said. Stitch scanned the covers. There was nothing to indicate its title, or contents. 'It's a kind of background and guide to the healing elements of the power,' Joe said. 'It's a bit abstract in places but if you stick with it, then you'll get something out of it I'm sure.'

Stitch stammered, 'Err... sure. Thanks.'

Joe smiled. 'No pressure. Take it or leave it. I might be wrong.'

He turned to leave, and a shiver ran through Stitch as he held onto the book with both hands. He turned his attention back to the fire, the smouldering embers mesmerising as they blurred at the edges through his tired eyes.

* * *

JAY WOKE, shivering. It was light enough to see, but the sun had not yet risen above the treeline. She turned over to see Sammy and Cassie draped over each other. She smiled to herself and looked over to the empty sleeping bag where she expected Stitch. She scanned the ridge for a sign of him but all was quiet.

She struggled to her feet and stretched, aching from a restless night on a chalk mattress. She clambered up the bank, slipping and catching her elbow on a flint and crying out. She tried again and made it to the top.

She rubbed her elbow. At the edge of the trees, Jay could see that Stitch was asleep on the ground next to a still smoking fire. She walked around the inner circle, still unable to cross the treeline. Since reaching the top of Highdown the night before, her powers had been confusing. They were tangled, indecisive. Her natural inclination was to bury them as deep as she could. To prevent them from creating that unsettling feeling, the glimmer of anxiety, and the risk of detection.

She stopped at a point along the treeline that her body told her was the entrance – an almost imperceptible communication, a fluctuation in the energy. As she crossed, the wind was taken out of her. She struggled to catch her breath, doubled over, her throat constricting. She couldn't contain the tangled thoughts, the bubbling powers. Visions came, and she shut them down one by one. Through the mind of sleeping Stitch, she saw the seven hooded figures with whom he'd spent the night. The energy of the inner circle was strong, coming in pulses from the floor. The solid earth, the stretching roots of the beech trees reinforcing the very foundation of Highdown, the teeming masses of life below the surface, in the trees, in the sky above them and out to the sea – all were connected.

It took a minute for Jay to compose herself, to steady her breathing. She pushed the tangles down and pressed on through the clearing to where Stitch lay. 'Hey.' She kicked gently at his foot. He groaned and shielded his eyes from the light, squinting. 'What are you doing sleeping up here?'

Stitch looked around himself as if trying to remember. He grunted, 'Pagan sacrifice.'

'Come on, let's go see if we can see the sea.' She headed towards the outer circle of trees. Stitch scrambled to his feet, brushed himself down and followed, limping like he had a dead leg. Jay stood gazing out to sea when Stitch stopped alongside her. She glanced at him. 'You look worse for wear.'

'What are we looking at?' he said.

'There it is,' Jay said, pointing.

'What?'

'Beach Lane Café.' The outline of the café was visible against the white of the sky, standing above the level of the sea front houses like a lifeboat station, on wooden stilts over the sand. Jay turned to head back to the others. 'Let's move,' she said to Stitch, who scampered after her.

18

J ust a few hours after Jay and the others had left
Highdown Hill, the Reader stood beside the
remains of the fire inside the ring of trees, kicking at
the charred lumps of wood.

At the summit of Highdown, the Reader, Marcus, stood
confused by what he sensed. He felt Jay, her power familiar
to him now. But there was more. Others. More than just her
friends. He felt an energy interacting with his, distorting
what he could see. But something else too, a boy, someone
in Jay's group with whom he connected. He felt frustrated;
he wasn't used to feeling confused. He kicked hard at a piece
of smoking wood, sending it fizzing across the clearing.

Two other Readers stood at the edge of the trees,
allowing Marcus his space, although he could hear their
every word as clearly as if he were standing right next to
them. Jimmy, the Reader responsible for taking Ben away,
and for failing to retrieve the notebook, turned to the man
next to him. 'You think he smells something, Drake?'

Drake nodded. 'It stinks of her up here. Would have

thought you'd connect better than any of us, since it was you she gave the slip.' Drake stepped away toward Marcus.

Jimmy followed. 'They caught me by surprise. It wasn't just the girl who had power. They were shielding.'

'You need to focus on finding her,' Marcus said as they reached him. Marcus turned towards the coast, sensing that Jay had gone south, away from the Downs and the hill forts. Drake and Jimmy sat beside the remains of the fire and Drake lit a cigarette from a half-burnt stick. Marcus looked out over the fields to the south, towards the sea. He clenched his fists and tried to suppress his growing frustration. Where was that girl?

A parade of soldier ants veered around his boot, repelled by him. The sun reflected off their shiny black bodies as more emerged from the grass, scuttling and bumping into each other.

Marcus remembered Jay as a baby in the pram at the bottom of the garden. He had little experience but she seemed a fussy baby, always interrupting as he and Sonia lay together. Those were lazy days, a different time, the summer just after his transformation. The affair ended less than a year after Jay was born. If he had known back then that the squawking little baby would grow to such strength, to such a threat... he could have ended it before it started. He shook his head to clear it. It didn't matter. Regrets were futile. Now was his time.

Marcus was the strongest Reader on the force. He knew of no one stronger and took pride in this fact. The only threat to his remaining the most powerful was the State's ability to reduce, and the possibility of reduction by a level eight Given. Jay would not be the one to threaten him. He would get to her long before she grew into her powers.

Marcus looked over his shoulder at his two colleagues

by the fire, arguing between themselves. His attention was drawn back to the sea, towards where he could see the Beach Lane Café in the distance. He looked down, kicked out at the ants at his feet and turned to walk south, back towards the car park.

19

A s Cassie pulled the Ford out of the Highdown car park, Jay turned to where she'd transcribed the words of the legend.

'Read it aloud, let's hear,' called Stitch from the back.

'It talks about a village at the confluence of rivers. That's the bit we've been getting to. It says the village was damned, cursed, and fated to die –

"In the rainy season, the rivers would swell and burst their banks, destroying houses and businesses. Many villagers left to settle in the surrounding areas. A sink-hole opened up to form a deep lake at the point of confluence of two rivers."

'Two? I thought it was three?' said Sammy.

'Hang on,' said Jay, 'it's coming –

"The sink-hole formed a reservoir, containing the flow from the rivers. Whilst only twenty metres across, the hole was said to stretch deep into the earth's core. At the pit, the villagers saw that a third, previously uncharted, underground river also flowed into the sink-hole. It was this unnamed river of unknown source that was said to bring luck and to lift the curse on the village."

'That's convenient,' said Cassie, turning onto the main road towards the coast.

Jay rolled her eyes and continued. 'It says –

"Some years later, there were three children, sisters, the youngest of whom was persecuted for her witchery. She was protected only by the guile and cunning of her two sisters who kept her safe, hidden from the church elders who pursued her, and would surely have put her on trial. On the warm afternoons of the summer, when the winds dropped, and the sun dipped in the sky, the sisters would break free of the village to explore the land to the north, where the rivers flowed so full of fish you could reach in and take them in your hands."'

'That's Dad's story,' said Sammy.

Jay nodded acknowledgement to her brother then continued –

' *"The youngest loved nothing more than to explore the rivers and flood plains with her sisters, and, truth be told, she was at one with that world. She had the feel of the waters, a sense of its inhabitants, its multitude of living things. The fish would come to her, and she would take them in her hands, whisper to them and return them to the water."'*

'The fish whisperer,' said Cassie.

' *"Not long after the sisters passed their eighteenth birthdays, they came across an unmapped river. A river that disappeared underground. Deducing that it must be the third source that fed their village lake, they built a log raft on which they navigated the river, emerging as they had suspected at the sink-hole lake, plunging beneath the water.*

As the sisters floated to the surface, only two figures appeared, soaked to the skin as they clambered up the side of the pool. The third sister was forever lost."'

'What happened to her?' asked Sammy.

'It doesn't say,' said Jay.

'"After a time, with the flow from the three rivers, the entire area sank deeper into the earth and the village became uninhabitable. It disappeared and was remembered as the Interland."'

Jay finished reading, and the four were quiet for a moment.

'What's up, Jay?' said Sammy.

She looked up from the notebook. 'I feel manic. Since Highdown. I can't seem to stop my powers from bubbling. And there's a Reader on to us and getting closer.'

'Is it the one who was at the house?' said Cassie.

'Someone stronger, and more than one of them.'

Stitch leaned between the front seats. 'We need to keep going. We won't be able to hide. The only thing we can do is stay ahead of them.'

'We need to *lose* them,' said Jay. 'If the Interland exists, we can't risk leading the Readers there.'

* * *

CASSIE PULLED INTO A PETROL STATION. Jay put unleaded in the car as the other three headed inside. Sammy picked a steak pie from the fridge and a bottle of water from the shelf. Stitch and Cassie argued over the merits of Dr Pepper versus Coke.

Sammy joined the queue behind a musty smelling man in a hi-vis jacket. He gave the man some room and looked out over the forecourt to where Jay was still filling the car. A van pulled into the space beside her, the driver getting out to fill the tank. The other man in the front of the van wound down his window to get a look at Jay. Sammy could see that he was speaking to Jay but that she was ignoring him, avoiding his eye.

Sammy smiled at his sister as she entered the shop. 'Making friends, sis?'

'Tossers.'

'What did they say?'

'Usual crap,' said Jay as Stitch joined them in the queue, his arms loaded with food. Cassie had almost as much, including a two-litre bottle of Dr Pepper.

'You two have enough sugar?' said Sammy.

Stitch displayed his goods. 'Enough for all of us,' he said.

'There she is,' said a man entering the store – the driver of the van.

'What's his problem?' Cassie said to Jay.

'Ignore him,' said Jay. Sammy's heart raced. The two men had joined the queue. In Sammy's experience, it was him and Stitch that people usually picked on when the four of them were together. For some reason, men thought that two males accompanying women were fair game for fighting. Winner takes the females. It was always Cassie that got them out of it. Sammy hadn't yet met any guys that Cassie couldn't see off.

The two men continued to make snide comments, smirking and eyeing Cassie who couldn't help but react. 'What you staring at?' she said through gritted teeth. The two men laughed and Cassie turned away from them. At the tills, the men finished paying while the cashier was still working through Stitch and Cassie's mountain of food. As they left, the bigger one brushed past Cassie and said, 'You want to see what I've got in my van, love?' before pushing out through the door. Cassie swung around and headed after him.

'Cassie,' called Jay. 'Leave it, we need to get going.'

Cassie ignored her friend and pushed through the door and after the two men. Sammy watched through the window. Cassie caught up with them as they reached their van. Sammy stared, a mix of admiration and fear for Cassie. 'Shit, Jay. What's she going to do? Those guys are big.'

'Don't worry about Cassie,' said Jay, helping Stitch to bag all their food. 'It's those men you want to be concerned for.'

As the three of them left the shop, Cassie was squaring up to the men, taking a fighting stance. One of the men laughed and turned to head back to his van as the other moved to shove Cassie. She dodged him and kicked out at his leg. He stumbled and turned to Cassie, shouting.

Sammy and Jay got in the car, Jay taking the driver's seat and starting the engine. As Cassie goaded the two men, Stitch disappeared around the back of their van. After a minute, Cassie left the men, shouting, and climbed into the car.

'Finished playing?' said Jay.

'They're not putting up much of a fight,' said Cassie.

'Let's go,' said Stitch, climbing into the back seat next to Cassie.

Jay pulled away as one of the men made as if he would try to get to them, changing his mind as Jay sped away. Through the rear windscreen, Sammy watched with a grin as they ran to the van and jumped in to make chase. 'They're following.'

'No they're not,' said Stitch, smiling. 'I let three of their tyres down. Would have done all four if we hadn't rushed off.'

Sammy and Jay laughed as Jay pulled into the flow of traffic and they continued towards Beach Lane Café.

20

The Café was a tired, glass-fronted building too far from the centre of town to attract tourists, but, nestled in the retirement centre of the south coast, made enough in afternoon teas to pay the rent. It sat on wooden columns, like stilts, over the stones. To get in you had to walk across the pebbles and up a flight of steps to the main doors. Windows stretched the full length of the building, providing every table a view of the beach.

Jay and Stitch walked straight to the back which displayed the local history. Cassie and Sammy ordered tea and chose a table at the window, far enough away from two elderly women sharing a pot of tea.

Jay and Stitch stopped at an old map tacked to the wall, studied it for a moment and then looked at each other. Jay pulled out her notebook, her fingers trembling with anticipation. There was a clear resemblance between her dad's sketch and what they were looking at on the wall.

'The second bow,' said Stitch, moving to the wall and tracing his finger along a line on the map to form a triangle from Highdown Hill, to the Castle at Bamber, and then on to a third location further along the coast. 'Where's this?'

'West Beach, Littlehampton,' said Jay, triumphant. 'That's our next stop. We need to get there and look across to see the trajectory… from here.' Jay pointed to the map. 'That's how we find the intersect.' Jay restrained herself from squealing and hugging Stitch.

'And that's how we find the gateway,' smiled Stitch.

Jay looked back to the map on the wall. 'If we're right. If there's a confluence of rivers at the intersection.'

'There will be. There has to be.' Stitch couldn't stop grinning.

A woman edged towards them with a tray holding two pots of tea and four cups, spilling tea onto the tray as she approached. Sammy went to help, taking the two teapots. The woman left the tray and returned to serve another customer.

'Who uses saucers these days?' said Sammy. 'What's wrong with mugs?' He slid the cups onto the table and mopped up the mess with a paper towel. Jay looked out at the sea, waves folding over each other and breaking where the pebbles turned to sand. She was glad to be inside, protected from the wind and the spray, the chapped lips and the earache.

Sammy sipped his tea and winced. 'Earl Grey. I asked for builder's.'

'Oh, just drink it anyway.' Jay smiled. She sipped her own drink, relieved that it was normal tea. A man came in with his Labrador and ordered a coffee. The woman spooned a measure of instant into a cup and topped it up with boiling water from the urn. Stitch and Cassie continued to explore the information boards.

'You think we've found it?' said Sammy. The woman

came back with slices of cake and Sammy tucked in with a plastic fork.

'There must be something more. Dad said it was the source of the power, and a gateway to somewhere we could be safe from the Readers.'

'What stops the Readers passing through the gateway?' said Sammy.

'Their power is drawn from a different source. So they can't enter. Only the Given, or people with no power, can enter. The Readers don't generate energy in the same way.' Sammy finished his cake and eyed Jay's. She pushed it towards him and he tucked in as she poured more tea. She took a sip, burning her top lip. Jay thought for a minute, looking back out of the window, over the pebbles to the retreating tide. Clouds gathered, and spits of rain on the window obscured the view. She thought of her mum. 'Reckon the old crow's going nuts?'

'Only when she realises there's no one to get her tea,' Sammy said. 'Jabba the Hutt without the slaves.' Jay felt an uncharacteristic pang of sympathy for her mother, picturing her as she realised she was all alone.

'You reckon we've picked up any of her genetic traits?' Jay said.

'Let's hope you've got the Jabba, and I've got the...' Sammy trailed off.

'Her drive,' Jay said. 'You've got her tenacity. When she gets the bit between the teeth, she won't let go. You have that, but you've turned it into a positive. You have a determination in you.'

Sammy sat back, puffing out his cheeks. He pulled back his sleeve a little. Nothing. He shrugged. 'You've definitely got some Dad in you,' he said. 'You two and your puzzle-powers.' He paused, thinking.

'What was it like, seeing him at the prison?' said Sammy.

'Bit weird to be honest, like we didn't know each other. All he really wanted to talk about were his plans.'

Stitch bumbled over to the table, knocking into it so that Jay's tea spilled. 'How far to West Beach?' he said as he and Cassie sat down.

'Half hour drive,' said Jay. 'I've walked it before. Nothing like walking the beach at dawn.'

'I'll take your word for it,' said Cassie.

Stitch took the teapot from Cassie and as he lifted it to pour, Jay felt a jolt in her chest as if her heart had stopped, as if the air had been sucked from her lungs.

The tea hung in the air between the spout and the tea cup. The bustle in the café died and her friends sat, frozen in time. Jay experienced a moment of deep clarity. She felt the heartbeat of the Reader as if it were beating in her own chest. She knew it was Marcus, the level eight. He was near, and he was coming. Jay glanced around the café. A wasp caught her eye, frozen in mid-flight near the window. As she stared, its wings came into focus, shimmering in the light. They twitched, then flapped, stopped, then flapped again like an old engine sparking into life. It hit the window, bouncing off and going again, trying to get through to the outside.

The world turned. The tea sloshed into the cup and the noise, chatter and rattling of crockery, returned. Jay stood, pushing her chair back so that it toppled onto the floor. She looked around the room, out through the window to the beach and behind her to the carpark. Nothing.

But he was close, she could feel him.

'What?' said Sammy.

'They're here.'

'Who?' said Cassie.

'Where?' said Stitch.

'Close. I don't know. But they're really close. We need to go right now.'

They scrambled to collect their belongings. Out of the café and onto the stones, they headed for the car park. Almost to the car, it happened again.

It was as if a blanket had been thrown over her world, silencing the seagulls, the wind and the waves. Her friends and brother stood motionless, in mid-stride, and mid-sentence. She stopped, stepped back towards Sammy and touched his face. His eyes were alive, but fixed and sightless. She turned back towards the car park. A man in black, some fifty yards from them, moved through the frozen time just as Jay did.

Jay recognised the shorter of the frozen men. Jimmy. The Reader. She knew that the man in motion was Marcus. The third figure was presumably another Reader.

As Jay sensed the world begin to turn once more, she spun around to face her friends and opened her arms to stop them in their tracks. Cassie and Sammy bundled into her, squawking their displeasure.

'This way, go, now,' Jay said, ushering them around the back of the café. 'They're coming across the car park.'

They turned to run. Cassie and Sammy led Jay and Stitch to a hiding place under the floor of the café, between the thick wooden stilts.

'We can't stay here,' said Stitch. 'They'll sense us. They'll sense Jay.'

Jay poked her head out around a wooden column to see that the three figures were moving towards the café. 'Too late,' she said. 'I'll shield. We can't move now.'

'They'll come after us,' said Stitch

'Cassie, you take Sammy and Stitch, go by road. Sammy

knows how to get to West Beach. But, Sammy, take an indirect route.'

'What about you?' said Sammy.

'I'll go the beach route. I'll have to divert up through the scrubland around Ferring but I know it well enough. They'll not be able to follow easily. And splitting up might confuse them.'

Sammy looked concerned. 'Are you sure? Why can't we all just…'

'No time, Sammy. Get to the car and move off east before doubling back to get to West Beach.'

The three men were climbing the wooden steps to the café door.

'They're in, let's go, around the back way.' Sammy, Cassie and Stitch made towards the car.

'Sammy,' called Jay in a loud whisper, then threw him the car keys. With this, Jay turned and ran towards the sea, not looking back, not wanting to allow Marcus to sense her. She ran until she was onto the sand, around the corner past the first breakwater and hidden amongst the hills of stones.

Someone was running towards her.

'Stitch!'

'I'm coming with you.'

'Why?'

'I'm coming, don't argue. Let's go.' He pushed past her and continued along the beach.

Jay was relieved to have Stitch with her, not for any reason she could make sense of, she just knew it was important for them to be together, in the same place. The tide was out past the sandbank and the beach was deserted. Jay decided they should walk along the wide stretch of wet sand between the stones and the sea. She felt safe closer to the water.

Whispers came over the breeze off the sea, whispers that were now familiar to Jay, and comforted her. The sand under her feet moved as she walked, squirming and squeezing as if helping her along. She imagined the lugworms buried there, leaving their little pyramid-like casts on the surface, the worms that she and her dad used to dig for to fill the bait box when they went fishing. Now they held her, supported her as she and Stitch made their escape from the Readers. For now, they were safe.

Breaking waves frothed over the beds of mussels in the distant shallows. The wind had dropped and after a few minutes walking, it was already warm enough to shed her hoodie. Stitch sparked up conversation from time to time but Jay couldn't formulate words, her mind scrambled by the events at the café. After a while Stitch gave up and they walked in silence.

21

The three men stood in the doorway to the café and looked around. The only people inside were two elderly women and a man with his dog. 'She was here,' Marcus said.

'Well she's not anymore. Which way?' said Jimmy, impatient.

Without a word, Marcus turned and descended the wooden steps. Back on the stones he made his way to the Land Rover, his mind distracted. A time freeze had happened to him just once before, on the day he was asked to read one of the prisoners no one else could break. She had been in custody for weeks, but was too powerful for the other Readers to contain. Marcus had been told to manipulate her to make her more agreeable. As he had approached the holding cells, the world around him had frozen, much like it had outside the café. The episode had made Marcus feel sick. It was as if his mind couldn't grasp what was happening and he shut down for a few minutes. When he had gathered himself, everything around him had returned to normal. But he couldn't carry on. He had to leave.

He'd always put the episode down to a psychological anomaly. A one-off. But now…

'What's wrong?' asked Jimmy.

'I can't talk about it,' said Marcus.

'Which way?' said Drake.

'I'm not sure,' said Marcus.

Jimmy sat forward in the back seat. 'What do you mean you're not sure? Which way? Tell me you know which way?'

Marcus couldn't get a fix on them. The signal was confused. 'They've split up.'

'Then we follow the girl,' said Drake. 'Which way?'

Marcus closed his eyes for a moment and then got out of the car. Jimmy and Drake looked at each other and then followed. Marcus led them back towards the café and onto the stones, heading for the sea. At the water's edge he stopped, looking along the line of the breaking waves towards the west.

'She's walking?' asked Jimmy.

'Two of them.'

'Let's go, they can't be far,' said Drake, starting along the sand but getting bogged down in the soft surface. The sand glooped and moved around his feet. As Jimmy made to step towards his friend, he too found his feet getting stuck.

Marcus took in a deep breath, drinking in the power of the girl, sensing its influence. 'Her power is growing,' he said.

Drake made his way out of the sand. 'You can feel it?'

'And something else. There's something in one of the others.'

'Power?'

'No.' Marcus tapped his own forehead with frustration. 'He's in here.'

'Then you can use him?' said Drake.

Marcus nodded, then closed his eyes. He focused on the connection. It took him just a few seconds to enter Sammy's mind but the connection was weak. Sammy had reached a safe distance, too far away for Marcus to use the full power of control and influence. 'I can't stop them.'

'Then let's go,' said Drake.

'Wait.' Marcus closed his eyes again. He focused again, entering Sammy's mind with force, digging through the consciousness and into the core. He squeezed as hard as he could before Sammy slipped out of range. 'Something at least,' he said.

'Good,' said Drake.

'We need to call in the others,' Marcus said.

Drake looked surprised. 'We don't need more Readers, surely. It's one girl.'

Marcus turned away from Drake. 'I told you. She's more than that, don't underestimate her power.' Marcus turned to see Jimmy still battling with the sinking sand. 'Not this way,' he shouted, 'we go by road.' With this he turned and made back up the beach towards the car park.

22

They stuck to the beach all the way through to Ferring, where the public roads veered north and the sea rolled up against private gardens. 'How can someone lay claim to the sand and the sea?' said Jay. 'Just how far out to sea does it belong to them?' Jay jumped the fence easily enough, daring anyone to try to stop her. Stitch remained quiet, twice looking over his shoulder then following close behind.

Across a stretch of scrubland, over a stile and into the eastern boundary of the tired and grey seaside resort of Littlehampton. Every August, the focus of the town was on cashing in on the seasonal rush. Harvest time. The arcades and the fairground rides pinned between the estuary of the Arun and the sea front hotels buzzed with life and creaked at the seams.

Jay watched Stitch as they walked. He was as close as family to her as you could get. Their sleeping together felt unresolved. There had been times when she wished they could be together, had those kinds of feelings for him, but it was too scary to think of killing what they had.

They stepped onto the wooden decking of the pier, into the footsteps of Jay's former self as a child, with her dad, and Sammy on a fishing trip. Little about the place had changed. Even the pastel blue paint on the wooden railings was the same, re-painted every spring in anticipation of the coming tourist trade. A group of kids fished off the end of the pier in her dad's old spot. Others dangled their orange crab lines over the sides, their buckets alive with pincers and claws.

'It's big, Dad, it's big,' said a little girl hauling up an impressively large crab. She pushed her dad away as he tried to help her guide it towards her bucket. 'I can do it, I can do it.'

From the end of the pier, Jay could see over the mouth of the river to the West Beach dunes rising above the river wall.

* * *

CASSIE DROVE IN SILENCE. Sammy searched his mind for something intelligent or funny to say. But neither felt appropriate, so he leaned his head against the glass and kept quiet, watching the hedges and trees flicker past.

'This whole thing's bullshit, don't you think?' Cassie said after a while.

'Huh?'

'These men in black, the legend...'

Sammy was surprised that Cassie continued to deny it, despite having her own connections to the place through her grandad. She had such fight and determination, but it came with a bitterness that hung over everything. 'Those men didn't look like bullshit to me.'

Cassie remained silent for a moment, her eyes on the road. 'You know, when we moved over this way from Amberley, me and Grandad wanted to stay. Last thing I wanted was to move. I spent my entire life in that area. It's where Grandad settled when he came over from Jamaica, and it's where he took me and Charlie trekking through the thicket.'

'To find the Interland? The Caverns?'

'It was all about exploring the thicket, the Amberley Wilds and all its life – the trees, birds.' She paused. 'I always hoped he'd take us to the Caverns.'

'Your grandad moved with you?'

Cassie nodded. 'He lasted less than a month before he went AWOL. I think the move broke him. He'd never lived anywhere but Amberley.'

They hit a T-junction and Cassie turned towards the coast. 'I remember Grandad talking about that woman, the one who got involved in the big protest. What was her name?'

'Zadie Lawrence,' said Sammy, remembering the unspoken information passing between his dad and Jay the day of the protest, a communication he now better understood.

'My grandad seemed to think she was the answer to everything, way before the protest.' Cassie laughed. 'She changed things alright. Didn't exactly get the freedom she fought for.'

'Maybe she hasn't finished yet,' said Sammy.

Cassie gave him a sideways glance then slammed the brakes. They jolted to a standstill and Cassie apologised as Sammy got his breath back, thankful to his seatbelt. Cassie let the engine idle a moment as she looked out and up towards the hills in the distance. 'Highdown looks a picture from this angle.'

Sammy looked up towards the peak. 'These hills always get me.' Cassie pulled away and an inexplicable lump formed in Sammy's throat. He swallowed and turned away from Cassie towards the window. As he did so, he felt a wave of nausea. His head spun and he let out an involuntary groan.

'You OK?' Cassie said as Sammy's head lolled and he tried to stop the horizon spinning in front of his eyes. It was like something was burrowing into his consciousness, digging and unbalancing his sense of reality.

'Spinning out,' said Sammy, unable to keep his eyes open. He leaned back in his seat. 'I need to close my eyes for a bit.' He fought to keep his thoughts from racing, struggling to hold on to his sense of reality. His mind raced in search of an explanation – he was ill, food poisoning, drugged, dying. A cold sweat came over him as a darkness descended, cloaking him in an oppressive, bitter depression.

* * *

THEY WAITED in the car in the gravel car park on West Beach. Sammy watched with his head up against the window as cars gradually left at the end of the day, crammed full of beach gear, kids with sunburned noses.

'They must be close,' Sammy said. His head had settled, but the nausea remained. He felt as if he'd had his mind spooned out – listless, and exhausted, no closer to understanding what happened, what was wrong with him. Cassie was slumped back in her seat, arms crossed.

'Not been here for years,' said Sammy. 'See the pier over the other side? We used to go fishing there with Dad. Don't think I ever caught anything except seaweed.'

'Are you alright now?' Cassie said, concern in her voice.

'I think so.'

'That River looks crazy,' Cassie said, peering through the

darkness at the swirling expanse of the Arun as it thrust out to sea.

'It's more dangerous than it looks. Not one to mess with.'

'Challenge accepted,' said Cassie. She opened the door and stripped off her jeans and top. Sammy stared open mouthed as Cassie threw her clothes into the back seat and scampered over the sand to the river wall where she leaned over the railing to see down to the river below. By the time he'd gathered himself to get out of the car, Cassie was already bounding along the river wall towards the sea, 'Bring the stuff,' she called over her shoulder.

The sea breeze was gentler on the west side of the river. Darkness approached as Jay and Stitch walked alongside the river wall, Jay fending off vertigo as she looked over the railings into the swirl below. The eddies around the posts of the river wall twisted and turned, nudging their way out to sea. The undercurrents along that section were strong, where the river became estuary and pushed towards France. She kicked a stone over the edge and watched as it disappeared without sound into the froth, an ingredient delivered to a witch's cauldron.

Up ahead, Jay heard familiar voices. Sammy shouted at Cassie to get down off the river wall, Cassie laughing back at him.

'Is that...?' said Stitch.

'Yep. God knows what she's doing.' Cassie strode along the river wall, stripped to her underwear. She was tall and stringy, her dark skin shimmering, braids swinging loose around her shoulders.

'What is she doing?' said Stitch. They heard Sammy call for her not to be stupid and to get down.

'Don't worry,' Cassie called back to Sammy, striding and picking up speed so that she was jogging along a wall no more than a foot wide, twenty feet above the river on one side and six feet above the sand on the other. It made Jay dizzy just watching. Sammy ran along the sand to keep up with her. Jay stopped atop the wall, watching Cassie's ballet-like gracefulness as she strode further out to sea. When she got to the point of the estuary opposite the pier on the east beach, Cassie slung a leg over the railing, then the other, to stand facing the river, her back to Sammy.

'Cassie, come on, it's too dangerous,' Sammy shouted.

'It's perfect,' Cassie shouted back. 'I'll catch up with you in the dunes. Go find Jay and Stitch.'

'Cassie!' Stitch shouted, but the wind threw his words back in his face and neither Cassie nor Sammy appeared to hear.

Sammy shouted, his voice carrying to Jay and Stitch on the wind, 'Come on, please...' but his words tailed off as Cassie threw herself forward, her sleek body bending into an elegant dive. Stitch's mouth dropped open. An onlooker screamed. Cassie was invisible as she flew through the air, against the charcoal canvas of the river, and Jay didn't see her hit the water through the gloom and turbulence of its surface.

'Crazy,' said Stitch.

Jay leaned over the river wall to catch a glimpse of Cassie. A seagull swooped across the surface as if searching for leftovers. Nothing but whirlpools and eddies. Panic rose in Jay's chest. She allowed her mind to open to the energy of the river as it pushed and jostled its way towards the sea, expanding in all directions. She sensed little but passing waves of whispers and silence. She pushed and prodded with her mind, drawing power from the water, refusing to accept its silence. A burst of energy sent a jolt through Jay's bones. The whispers grew. She turned to Stitch, half expecting to see him knocked off his feet by the energy she felt flowing from the river. He stood firm, his eyes fixed on Jay. He'd felt something too. Jay turned back to the river, the streamlines becoming more visible in her mind's eye. Discernible and defined they wrapped themselves around the whispers, and around Cassie. Through the gloom, the water seemed to open to Jay, and Cassie became visible, her body wrapped in layers of the river like a baby swaddled.

The whispers came, growing to a wall of white noise. Jay filtered, ordered and arranged until the connection became firm, and it was she, Jay, who held the power of the water. She was in control. Mischievous currents nipped at Cassie, tugged at her limbs and dragged her down, but Jay guided her through the channel of the estuary and clear of the undercurrents. The white noise dampened to whispers, coming and going on the breeze. Cassie was safe.

'Come on,' said Jay. 'Let's help Sammy with those rucksacks.'

Stitch shook his head and tore his eyes away from the gloom of the river to catch up with Jay who was already calling after her brother as he battled to carry two rucksacks. 'What about Cassie?' he said.

'She's fine now, she's safe,' said Jay. They took the back path up past the drinks kiosk, and into the section of dunes between the sea and the golf course. Jay and Sammy took off their shoes and socks, Jay wanting to feel the cold wet sand between her toes. Jay figured that they could get to the high point in the dunes and see all the way back towards Highdown and Bamber.

Sammy was quiet as they walked. He looked tired. His

face was pale with dark rings around his eyes. 'Are you OK?' Jay asked, trying to get a better look at him.

'I'll be fine. It's been a weird day. Something took the wind out of me back there but I feel better now.'

Jay could hear music and laughing and was pulled towards its source. West Beach was where people gathered, the kind of people that spent the summer sleeping under the stars, or in little one-man tents, some of them with surf boards, though the surf was rarely any good. As they got closer, Jay could see the orange flicker of a fire and people, in groups of three or four. They parked themselves in the sand, on the periphery but close enough to feel the warmth from the fire, and offloaded their bags. Stitch and Sammy flopped down on the sand, Stitch starting to roll a cigarette.

As Jay pinpointed the highest section of dunes for a vantage point, Cassie emerged from the darkness. The rest of the party goers stopped and stared.

'Took your time,' Sammy said.

'Worried?'

'No,' Sammy said, lying back in the sand.

Jay stood, handing Cassie a towel. 'That river can be lethal,' she said, emphasising her serious tone.

Cassie held Jay's eye. 'I had it covered,' she said.

'I'm heading up there.' Jay pointed. 'To check on this second bow.' She picked the notebook from her rucksack and Sammy stood to join her. Together they climbed the dunes to the high point.

'That's Bamber Castle.' Sammy pointed. In the distance, they could see the light from the castle illuminating its turrets, some six miles east of their location.

'And there's Highdown.' Jay pointed towards the Downs.

'Where?'

'The glimmer up on the hill, a fire. And...' Jay continued, 'yes! There is the trajectory, the arrow.'

'Don't see it,' said Sammy.

'The line of streetlamps from the castle, with the trees. That's the boulevard that runs north from the castle, down to where your old school is. See it?'

'Is that the trajectory of the arrow?'

'Reckon so.'

'Then it's easy to plot, I know that road.'

MOST OF THE beach partiers were drinking from bottles and cans. A guy with a beard down to his chest was setting up a barbecue. He squirted lighter fluid over the charcoal to kick things off, leaning back to keep his beard away from the flames. An older man in a tattered anorak and beaten shoes, largely ignored by everyone else, wandered from group to group to scab a smoke or a drink. He settled next to the fire, cross-legged on someone's rug, gazing into the flames.

'Look,' said Stitch. 'See what you've done.' In the distance, the flashing lights of a coastguard boat patrolling the estuary reflected off the surface of the water. Cassie shrugged and continued to pull on her clothes before settling down on the sand. She riffled through her rucksack and took out her sleeping bag, rolling it out to sit on after pulling two bottles of red wine from inside.

A boy with blonde dreadlocks approached. 'Where are you guys from?' he said, though clearly was speaking only to Cassie.

Cassie looked away, disinterested, until the boy handed her the remains of a joint. She stared at it a moment, smiled, and took it.

'From around here.' Cassie nodded in the general direction of the river. 'We're on a quest,' she said, coughing as she exhaled. Sammy turned to Jay and rolled his eyes. They laid out their sleeping bags.

Stitch squeezed in next to Jay. 'Tell me then. What could you see from up on the dunes?'

'We got it, Stitch,' said Sammy. 'Home and dry. Just need to plot it out on the map.' As Sammy spoke, his head lolled and he had to put out a hand to steady himself.

'You OK?' said Stitch.

Sammy shook his head clear, blinking. 'Dizzy spells. Not feeling too special. I'll be OK. I probably need to eat something.'

Jay looked over at her brother. 'Grab something from the rucksack, and have some water. Then rest, OK?'

'Yes, boss.' He smiled.

Stitch turned to Jay. 'So you think you know where it is?'

'We'll see, tomorrow,' said Jay. 'As long as we stay ahead of the Readers.'

Stitch grabbed one of Cassie's bottles of wine, took a swig and handed it to Jay.

'I used to know people down here,' Jay said, glancing at the faces around the fire. 'Not anymore. Did you know that this is a nudist beach by day?' Jay smiled at Stitch.

'No.' Stitch laughed.

'Seriously. If you come down here in the day, you'll see people in the dunes, naked blokes standing with their hands on their hips like mannequins. We used to bring the dog down here sometimes when I was a kid. Scared the crap out of me when I walked straight into a bloke standing stark naked.'

Stitch laughed.

It grew darker, and when the lights from the fairground

finally died, the stars emerged with distinction. Cassie had crashed out and dreadlock-boy had moseyed off elsewhere. Sammy was already asleep. Jay and Stitch lay back in the sand, spotting the different constellations and giggling, the effects of the wine loosening their mood.

'So tomorrow's the day?' Stitch said.

'Could be,' said Jay.

The sound of deep breathing came from Sammy's direction. 'You think he's OK? Seems a bit off.'

'Been a bit of a day. I'm sure he'll be fine,' said Stitch.

Cassie let out a snort followed by steady snoring. Stitch laughed. 'Sammy and Cassie have been pretty tight,' he said.

'They have a connection,' Jay smiled. 'Cassie seems more chilled with Sammy than with anyone else.'

'She's bailed us out of a few scrapes.' Stitch lay back on his sleeping bag, turning onto his side towards Jay so that they were close enough for her to feel his warmth. He pulled out a book.

'What are you reading?' asked Jay.

'Too tired to read,' Stitch said, pushing the book into his sleeping bag and yawning again. He closed his eyes.

Jay took a final swig of the wine, emptying the bottle, then pulled her rucksack towards her and picked out the Sasha Colden book.

Jay picked up the story where she'd left off at the bookshop. By the flicker of the fire, her eyes flowed over the words with ease, and she became drawn deep into the story, to a place beyond the pages. With each paragraph, each page, her sense of connectedness with the earth, and the sea, strengthened. The sand shifted beneath her body, cradling her. The whispers from the sea whirled and looped through the dunes on the wind. Alf came into her mind, then disappeared with the whispers.

Feeling protected, she lay back on the sand and closed her eyes for what felt like the first time in days.

24

Something woke Jay less than an hour later. She'd not been asleep for long, the party still going strong around them. As she turned to check on the others, she saw a man crouching over Cassie, one knee resting in the sand. Her heart punched at her chest, her senses heightened, face tingling with anxiety. She froze, holding her breath. The man was not much older than her. He was tall, solidly built, with dark skin. His expression was one of sorrow, or pity. He gazed at Cassie as she slept.

Jay calmed herself, forced a steady breath. This man didn't look or feel like a threat. 'Hey,' said Jay, keeping her voice low. The man snapped his head up. He held a finger to his lips as he stood, taking a step towards Jay and then veering off towards the sea. He nodded for Jay to follow.

She pushed herself off the sand, careful not to nudge Stitch or Sammy. She hurried after the man, stumbling as she tried to gain traction on the dry sand. As she reached the edge of the pebbles, she looked up to see his silhouette as he stood at the water's edge, his back to her so that his athletic frame was in sharp contrast to the surface of the water, shimmering in the light of the moon. She stopped short, taking a moment to read whatever she could in quick bursts to avoid detection.

The man was a Given. He opened up long enough to show Jay that he was on her side. He had brought a message of support, encouragement, if nothing more. He came to see Cassie too. To see her, but not for her to see him.

'Hi,' said Jay, standing alongside him.

'Reuben,' he said. 'Nice to finally meet you, Jay.'

'Finally?' said Jay, turning to him as he continued to stare out to sea.

'I've missed this.' He nodded towards the water. 'It's the sounds and the smells as much as what you see, don't you think?'

'I guess,' said Jay, trying her best to relax and not scream the many questions swirling in her mind. She knew he meant no harm, and she knew that he came to offer support, not resistance.

'Sorry. I just needed a minute there. The last time I saw the sea was about a year ago. Well, *exactly* a year ago as it happens.' He turned to Jay with a broad smile.

Before he could speak again, Jay twigged. 'You're the Reuben who Cassie grew up with.'

He looked surprised. 'You read that from me?'

'Not everything I figure out is by snooping in people's heads. Some knowledge can be gained the old fashioned way.' Jay returned her own gaze to the sea, a breeze picking up and churning the surface as the waves broke in front of them. 'Cassie told me about her lifelong friend since she was a baby. Her soul mate. The boy who moved away and never stayed in touch. Her best friend.'

Reuben hung his head, shifting the sand with the toe of his boot. 'That's a long story. I hope to be able to explain it to Cassie myself one day.'

'She's just over there.'

'Not today. Not now. I can't. I'm here because I've been tasked with bringing you a message. I can speak only to you. I am forbidden to talk to any without powers. Only to the Given.'

Jay snorted a laugh. She couldn't help but feel cynical, couldn't help the frustration she felt in the face of half-truths, cryptic messages and the uncertainty that seemed to surround everything associated with the Interland. 'Forgive me for not jumping for joy. I don't even know what I'm doing here.'

'There's a good reason, and I think you know that. I don't see that you have a choice.'

'There are always choices.'

'Not for you.' Reuben's tone was firm. 'And especially not with Readers. If they get to you, then that will be it for you and your friends. You don't think they'll simply put you in a nice holding camp and give the rest of them a slap on the wrists?'

'Well then? What message, who from?'

'They said I can't fill your head with too many facts about where you are trying to get to, for obvious reasons.'

'Not that obvious.' Jay frowned.

'Because of the Readers. They are powerful. If you have details, then they can take them. Marcus is a level eight, he could take information from any one of you and you wouldn't even sense it happening.'

Jay pictured the man in the car park. His two colleagues frozen in time but him still moving. 'I've seen him,' she said.

'Where?'

'Back that way.' She nodded down the beach. Reuben shifted on his feet and seemed to flinch a little. 'It's OK, we lost him. He's still on us but he's not close.'

'Can you tell when the Readers are close?'

'Sometimes.'

'That's something. Look, I've been asked to say nothing more than to give you confidence that you are on the right track.'

'So it's at the intersect?'

'I can't say any more. It could put you in more danger and hinder not help. And it could expose the rest of us to great danger.'

'Rest of us?'

'I've missed Cassie.' For a moment Reuben was silent, staring out to sea. Then, 'You can tell her I was here.'

'What do I say? "Hey, Cass, your old mate Reuben was here last night, popped in on his broomstick but I can't tell you why". You know Cassie, do you think that'll go well?'

'I want you to tell her about her grandad.'

'He's alive? He's in this place, the Interland?'

'He's the one who found it. He was custodian of the gateway. He never went through to the Interland, always remained on the outside, watching over it. Cassie's grandad was the one who brought me to the Interland when I turned 18. That's why I was never able to contact Cassie. I didn't abandon her. I didn't know about my power back then, not until the marking showed itself.' He pulled back his sleeve to reveal the number seven.

'But Cassie's grandad knew. He helped me. Introduced me to the underground.'

'Why not Cassie too?'

'She was young. And there was no power in Cassie that her grandad could see. Has she developed any marking since she turned eighteen?'

'Not that I know of,' Jay said. 'What about her grandad? Has he got abilities? Where is he?'

'He's a level four. But he didn't know until he was much older. The mark never came through for him until he passed 60. So now he's gone underground. He's moved from front of house to back of house if you see what I mean.'

Even Cassie's parents assumed that her grandad was dead. How would she ever explain this to Cassie? 'Why are you here, Reuben?'

'To bring a message, like I said. To give you confidence. You can do this. You are close.'

'And to give me a message that will both give my friend Cassie hope and break her heart?'

'There was no other way.'

Jay's frustration grew but she covered it with questions. 'So what happens when we get to the gateway? Will the others be able to pass through to the Interland?'

'Everything's changed. The Interland has grown. The surface world has moved so far in the wrong direction. We must get as many of the Given to a safe place as we can.'

'But I can't just leave my family, my friends.'

'You know that all of you have some level of power? Not just you.'

'What?'

Reuben smiled. 'We think so. Look, you don't have time to waste. You have to remain a good distance ahead of the Readers. Get to the Interland.'

'Where is it?'

'You know where it is.' He turned and started for the dunes.

'Hey,' said Jay. 'We will see you then?'

'I think it's inevitable. We've been waiting for you for a long time.' As Jay watched, he broke into a jog, picking up speed and disappearing into the dunes.

25

I n a northern suburb of London, on the outskirts of a residential area that stretched into affluent districts close to the city, the prison towered high above a surrounding patch of industrial land. In the exercise yard out the back, Ben and Matchstick sat apart from the other prisoners, or *customers*, as the authorities referred to them. It was important the institution retain some pretence of what it pretended to offer—rehabilitation and education—not what it truly offered, incarceration.

'We go out with a delivery vehicle,' Matchstick said, nodding towards the security gate where a truck idled. Two guards inspected the vehicle, the back doors of the truck open and its insides under scrutiny.

'I think those Readers would have something to say about that,' said Ben, not yet buying into Matchstick's confidence. He sensed that Jay had already left home and begun making her way through the hills, pursued by Readers. If Ben was to be true to his word, he needed to get out, and soon.

'That delivery bay marks the line between this bit,'

Matchstick motioned around himself, 'and the *education* section.'

'And *rehabilitation* beyond that. We need to move. We've been here long enough.' Every one of the 'customers' knew *rehabilitation* was where they sucked the last bit of resistance out of the Given, in a windowless room in the third and final wing of the prison.

'The *Sub Levels*. A small step from release,' Matchstick mused. 'Once educated, rehabilitated and released, we are no longer a disbenefit to society.' He paused, looking at Ben. 'For most, that might be a goal worth pursuing. True freedom from *rehabilitation*.'

Ben sighed. 'I used to think that freedom came from keeping under the radar.'

'A friend of mine, Luke, tried getting out in one of those vans,' Matchstick said. 'We were planning to go together, but I bottled it.' Matchstick thought for a moment, then said, 'We'd been planning it for a while but I got a bad feeling and tried to persuade him to wait a bit. He insisted. He wouldn't stay another night. So he went for it on his own.'

'How do you know he didn't make it?'

'Saw them take him. One of the Readers sensed he was there I reckon, by the way they searched the truck. It was a laundry truck. They had almost everything out on the road before they eventually found him hidden in the back.'

'What happened to him?'

'No idea. He never came back. There were rumours he'd moved on to *education*, which made no sense. The only people that move to *education* are the ones that are toeing the line, meeting their objectives. Not Luke. He was the opposite.'

'So they moved him to another prison?'

'If he was lucky.'

Ben watched the delivery truck at the gate. The guards closed the back doors and banged on the side to signal the all clear. The barrier rose, and the truck pulled out onto the perimeter road. 'I'm not feeling fully confident in your escape plan,' said Ben.

Matchstick laughed. 'My point is, I have developed an upgrade that might work, if we learn from where Luke went wrong.' Matchstick ambled towards the perimeter fence.

'I'm listening,' Ben said.

'To help shield from Readers, we need to put as much dense material as possible between them and us, yes?'

'Yes,' said Ben.

'I used to drive a delivery truck. There's no point in hiding in the back, we need more metal between us. I know the underside of those trucks like the back of my hand.'

* * *

BEN JOINED the queue in the dining room, a few people behind Matchstick. They found an empty table and sat, neither of them touching their food.

'We should eat,' said Matchstick, forking some spaghetti. Ben nodded and tucked in, forcing down the food down despite his nerves. He'd brought his belongings from his cell – a book, and a picture of Jay and Sammy.

'There are three trucks in the delivery bay,' said Matchstick. 'One of them is the type I used to drive. We need to get to that one before it moves out.'

Ben made to stand and Matchstick put a hand on his arm. 'Give it ten minutes.' Ben finished as much of his food as he could stomach and pushed away his tray. He drank the remains of his water and shifted in his seat. The minutes ticked by. Matchstick nodded.

Outside the dining hall they passed a guard and nodded a greeting as they made towards the exercise yard. There were no delivery drivers or guards in the loading bay as Matchstick had predicted. They crouched and made their way around the back of the loading bay to the truck. The back doors were open and Ben took a look inside. 'It's full of laundry,' he said.

'We won't be shielded in there.' Matchstick ducked down to inspect the underside of the truck. 'Follow me.'

Ben pushed himself along on his back as if he were preparing to service the truck. Matchstick had already folded himself up into the small cavity next to the fuel tank. 'There's no room!' Voices approached. Matchstick motioned for Ben to climb into the space between the exhaust pipe and the engine block, pushing himself up from the floor.

The truck rocked as its driver climbed into the front. Matchstick urged Ben on, reaching an arm out for support. As Ben squeezed himself into the impossible gap, breathing in Matchstick's stale odour as he pushed up against his bony body, the truck's engine started and the voices were drowned as the driver put the truck in gear and released the clutch. The only way Ben could keep from falling to the ground was to rest both feet on the vibrating exhaust pipe, bending it precariously.

With a thick waft of noxious fumes, the truck moved towards the exit and Matchstick shifted against Ben's knee. Ben's foot slipped, his leg dislodged and dragged against the rough gravel road, twisting, his trousers tearing, his skin shredding against the stones. Stifling a cry, he kicked up to rest his foot back on the exhaust pipe as the truck came to a stop at the exit gate. The engine died.

Footsteps. 'Something smells weird back there.' Ben could tell it was the voice of a Reader. It exuded arrogance.

His words came slowly and deliberately. He paced around the vehicle and opened the back,

'Dirty washing,' said the driver. 'That's your smell.'

'It's not the truck. Something else. Wait here.' The Reader stepped away and into the security hut. A minute later he came back and asked the driver to step out of the cab. Ben held his breath.

The Reader climbed up into the cab of the truck, sounding like he was rifling around in the passenger seat and searching through the glove box before he stepped back onto the tarmac. 'OK?' asked the driver. The Reader gave no response but instead paced the full perimeter of the truck, arriving back at the driver's door. He crouched, looking under the vehicle.

Ben held tight. Seconds ticked by. The engine of the truck sparked into life, and with a double-tap on the side of the vehicle, the driver edged the truck forward. Ben sensed the power of the Reader as they passed the security hut. He kept still, closing his eyes, shielding, and breathing through the pain in his arms. His feet began to warm on the exhaust pipe. Matchstick lowered his head below the level of the fuel tank to see the road ahead. He nodded at Ben and shouted in his ear above the noise of the engine and the tyres on the road, 'Ready?'

The truck's brakes squealed as they pulled up at a T-junction, the prison still visible in the distance behind them. Darkness closed in, red lights reflected in puddles on the road. The truck slowed, Ben dropped, slipped onto his front and rolled towards the pavement. Without looking back he launched himself across the path and into the darkness of an alleyway just as the traffic light turned green. No sign of Matchstick. He crouched to look under the truck. Matchstick was trying to untangle his sleeve from around the fuel tank mounting. He glanced at Ben just as the truck's engine raced and its wheels began to turn. Matchstick fell, was dragged, his shirt ripped, leaving him on his back in the middle of the road as the truck pulled away. He stood, grinning widely as the truck disappeared out of sight, then he strolled over to the alleyway to join Ben as if nothing had happened.

The street was quiet. A car passed, its windscreen wipers clearing the fresh rain that had started to fall, the sound of its tyres in the wet reminding Ben of home.

26

'You take the corners like you're driving a go-kart, and stop signs are not supposed to be optional.' The Ford crunched at every gear change, only increasing Jay's moaning, reminding Cassie of her grandad teaching her to drive, warning her how she'd strip her gears if she didn't soften the transition with the right revs.

Cassie's grandad was her last surviving grandparent before he disappeared two years ago. Cassie's brother Charlie had complained they shouldn't be having a funeral when he might be alive. But he must have died. Cassie could consider no reason he'd be alive and not have made contact. Before that, the boy she had thought of as a friend for life had moved away and vanished. The person she had planned to marry, in all the seriousness and depth of a love that began at six years old.

'Grandad never called it the Interland,' Cassie said to Jay as they rounded a corner at speed.

'It's a loaded word,' said Jay. 'Links to the legend and all the myth that surrounds it.'

'I guess,' Cassie said. The events of the past two days had

started to convince Cassie that her grandad's old stories, his descriptions of the magic of the caverns, had to be connected with Jay's Interland. The big confusion in Cassie's mind was where truth crossed into fantasy and wishful thinking.

'You used to live in this area?' said Jay.

'I did,' Cassie said. If her grandad had known the whereabouts of the caverns, the Interland, he never spilled. 'We used to go walking a lot. I always thought he was taking me to the Caverns, but he never did.' They would walk for miles, sometimes for hours at a time. Her grandad was always in control of the route, and the timing, always knew where they were, never lost.

'Did you ask him to?' Jay said, as Cassie took a roundabout like it wasn't there, causing Stitch and Sammy to pile up against Sammy's door.

'He said his memory wasn't all that. After a while I stopped asking. But I never gave up hoping, expecting that one day on one of our walks we'd just arrive there.'

'What about Reuben, did he walk with you?'

Cassie gave Jay a sideways glance. 'He came sometimes, why?'

Jay shrugged. Cassie took her eyes off the road to give her a look. 'I thought my grandad might be testing me, waiting until I was ready for something.'

'Waiting for you to come of age?'

'He waited too long, silly old bugger.'

They were quiet for a minute, Cassie concentrating on the winding road. Fields of green and yellow separated by low hedges and fences. They stopped at a T-junction.

'I miss him,' said Cassie.

'I know,' said Jay.

'Left,' came a shout from Stitch in the back, the road

map open on his lap. Cassie pulled out, tightened her grip on the steering wheel and jammed her foot to the floor.

* * *

THEY PULLED into the Barley Mow so they could rest, have a drink and study the maps. Stitch opened the car door and sloped towards the entrance of the pub, stretching back his shoulders as he walked.

'Shall we?' Cassie nodded towards the dark red door where a sign indicated the saloon bar. Stitch pushed through and the others followed.

They found a quiet spot in the pub garden overlooking a stream. Cassie spread the map on the table. 'Right, wonder woman,' she said. 'Where is this place?' Jay looked at Cassie and thought of Reuben. She flattened down the map, taking her time to get her bearings, looking from the map to their surroundings and judging their orientation by positioning the stream they were sat next to, the pub, and the road.

'This stream,' Jay said, 'connects into the Rother, just here...' She pointed at the map, Cassie and Stitch squinting to see. 'Then if you follow the Rother to here... it joins with the Arun.'

'Is that it?' Cassie looked up.

'Just south of there is where our two lines intersect.'

'The Gateway?'

'It's our best bet,' said Jay.

'But there's nothing there. That is the definition of the middle of nowhere. There are no roads, or tracks, paths or anything. That is right in the middle of the Amberley Thicket, do you know what that stuff is like?'

Jay shook her head. Cassie took a drink of her cider. 'The woods through there are thick and unmanaged. If you try to walk through there, you quickly get tangled in the overgrown brambles, bracken and everything else. There's a reason it's called "The Wilds". You'd need a JCB.'

'There must be some way,' Jay said. 'Dad said...'

'Your dad never actually went there,' Cassie interrupted. She sighed. 'There are infinite points that you *could* start from, but all of them are a good few miles out from that point.' She slumped back down onto the seat of the rickety picnic table. 'Can't you zone in or something, Jay? We could be walking out there for days and find nothing.'

'Where's your sense of adventure, Cassie,' said Sammy. 'Just because it won't be easy, doesn't mean we can't do it, right Jay?'

Jay looked again at the map and leaned in closer. 'Dad talked about a route along the Arun.' She pointed to a section of the Arun further upstream that ran down from the Black Rabbit pub. 'He described this place, further up, where the Arun widened alongside cattle fields, and poppy fields.'

'Poppies?' Cassie huffed.

'Maybe,' said Jay, uncertain. She continued moving her finger along the map, working her way down-river from the north, along the Arun. 'Like... here.' She pointed to a spot just east of where they had pinpointed the gateway, a place that was labelled *Sidwell*.

'That's not where the rivers meet,' said Sammy. 'And it's not at the intersection.'

Cassie said, 'It could be a starting point.'

'Worth a try,' said Jay, running her finger along an imaginary line between Sidwell and the intersection.

* * *

THE VILLAGE of Sidwell offered nothing but a string of disused farm buildings and a dilapidated church. The road petered out. Cassie squeezed the car up a track for a mile before it reduced to a narrow path. She reversed into a field, hiding the car behind a high hedge. They packed up their rucksacks, attached the two tents and continued on foot.

There were no footpaths or bridleways on the Ordnance Survey map so they walked blind, following their noses and taking the route that looked most plausible. Stitch and Sammy led the way through the trees, Cassie preferring to hang back with Jay. According to the map, they were less than two miles from the point of intersection, and Cassie was surprised that the going was so good – no distinct pathways, but the undergrowth between the trees was passable and they moved at a good pace.

Sammy and Stitch stamped down the stinging nettles, allowing Cassie and Jay an easy route in their slipstream. Cassie stole a glance at Jay. 'You OK?' she said, pulling Jay from her thoughts.

'Sorry. Miles away. I'm worried, what are we doing here?'

Cassie linked arms with her friend. 'The only thing we *can* do. Get somewhere safe, away from your stalkers.'

'I've dragged you all into this dangerous world.'

'Whether you like it or not, your world is our world. You think we should have stayed back home and carried on as if nothing was happening? This has been coming for some time.'

'It's not you they want, Cassie.'

'Not yet. Now it's the Given, it's you, your dad, others. But who's next? Another go at immigration? I remember my parents hopelessly trying to defend the rights of my grandad to stay in this country. It was like arguing with a wall. No sense of logic, or compassion, or even law.'

'They succeeded though?'

'Only after he got ill from all the stress and worry. Reckon that was the last straw for him. Wasn't long after that he went walkabout, died in the woods somewhere, probably. Then the letter came that he was given right to remain. Too little too late for Grandad. Stupid old bastard.' Cassie smiled. 'Anyway, I was thinking it's surprising to see you so far from your comfort zone. I was expecting a spaz-out before now?'

'I know. The anxiety is right up there, but there's something holding it back.'

'Thought you were on edge. You getting those things... what is it you used to call them? The thoughts that come into your head?'

'Pop ups,' Jay said.

'Yeah, that's it. Are they coming back?' Jay would become distressed in class, or when they were out somewhere. She'd get anxious and wind herself up so tight that there was nowhere for the tension to go but to explode into some kind of panic attack. And it always started with a simple thought that she couldn't close down.

'Not like before. They're in my head sometimes, but I can ride it. I'm better at it than I was back then.'

Jay reached to push a light branch out of her way and ducked under a more substantial one. 'To be honest,' Jay said, 'I don't think I ever really figured that stuff out. I just got better at managing it.'

The undergrowth thickened. Sammy used a stick to hack at thorny brambles and Cassie and Jay stamped through. Stitch and Sammy stopped and turned to Jay, Cassie a step behind her. 'Let's rest,' said Stitch, nodding towards a clearing by a fallen tree.

'How far away you think we are?' Cassie said.

'Difficult to tell. Maybe a mile,' Jay said as she sat back on the log next to Cassie. 'Might not sound like far, but at this rate it's a good couple of hours hacking through.'

A small bird flitted from a branch and settled on the log next to Sammy. It was no bigger than a mouse, tilting its head to the side and regarding him. On its head, a red-brown streak flowed from its eyes and merged into shades of brown and beige in the feathers that formed its wings.

'What is it?' Stitch said.

Cassie put a finger to her lips. 'Shh, it's a bird.'

'A sparrow,' Sammy whispered. The bird hopped closer along the log and Sammy held out a hand. The bird twitched its head to check the location of the other three people, then back to Sammy. It hopped onto the back of his hand.

Cassie sucked in a gasp, leaning closer to Sammy and the little bird. Sammy didn't seem surprised, then he glanced up as a flutter of sparrows streamed through the trees to rest on the log beside him, on his arm, his shoulder. One landed on Cassie's shoulder, though it lifted off when she let out a muffled scream. The sparrows fussed around Sammy in a cloud before, as quickly as they'd arrived, they streaked away into the sky with squeaks and flapping wings.

'Tell me I didn't just imagine that?' said Stitch, righting himself on the log then standing to look up into the trees after the birds. Jay stood to join him. 'That was a bit strange,' she said.

'Strange?' said Cassie, standing. 'It looked like Sammy and those birds were having a moment.'

'Sparrows,' Jay said.

Stitch nudged Sammy. 'Did that bird... like... say something?'

Cassie laughed. 'Come on, Stitch. Seriously.' She looked at Sammy. 'Tell me you're not talking to the birds, Sammy?'

Sammy smiled. 'Not *talking* to them, exactly.'

'Let's move,' Cassie said, 'before this gets any more Hitchcock.'

* * *

SAMMY AND STITCH led the way again. Jay put a hand on Cassie's arm to slow her down.

'What?' said Cassie.

'I need to tell you something.'

Cassie waited for Jay to continue. 'Someone came to give us a message last night, on the beach when you guys were asleep. Someone from the Interland.'

'Seriously? What message?'

'It was Reuben. He's a Runner. He's been on the other side, in the underground, ever since he disappeared. He's a level seven.'

Cassie's expression froze as the information sunk in. She smiled, then frowned. 'This is a joke, right?'

Jay shook her head. 'There's more.'

Cassie raised her eyebrows and Jay told her about what Reuben said about her grandad, carefully talking through every detail as Reuben had relayed it to her. Cassie listened in silence and eventually her legs gave way and she sat cross-legged on the floor of the woods. Sammy and Stitch pressed on, their chattering voices still audible in the distance.

Jay sat on the floor with Cassie and took her hands.

'Why didn't they contact me?'

'Reuben said it wasn't an option, or they would have been in touch sooner. It's only now, with the changes that are happening, and with you turning 18, that they have been able to reach out. He said that they're looking forward to you coming in.'

'You kept it from me all day? You know what they meant to me. How could you...'

'I didn't know how to tell you, how to explain.'

'So it exists. For real. It's not just you and your dad gone all magical. This place is for real?'

'Seems that way.' As Jay said these words, there came a scream from the direction of Sammy and Stitch. Cassie and Jay looked at each other, then shot to their feet, careering through the woods after the others.

* * *

STITCH AND SAMMY hung on to the edge of a hole in the woodland floor, like they'd fallen into a hidden animal trap, the ground a deep hole beneath them.

Jay lurched for Sammy's hand. For a moment, Cassie and Jay struggled to pull the boys out of the hole but they were too heavy. They clung with all their strength. Jay's right foot slipped. Stinging nettles ravaged her arm. Sammy's wrist slipped through her hand, sweat lubricating. Jay's muscles could take no more. Sammy fell, Stitch with him. They screamed in harmony as they crashed through the branches and into free fall. Jay could see nothing but the parted undergrowth and the white of a cliff face.

The girls heard a distant splash, then another. Then nothing. Jay looked at Cassie then to the hole in the floor of the forest. Cassie nodded. They held hands and took a deep breath before stepping into the hole.

PART IV

CONNECTED

27

J ay hit water a moment after Cassie. Turbulence, bubbles. Jay couldn't tell which way was up. Her skin screamed with pain from the impact and from the cold. Her lungs burned, aching for air. Exhausted from trekking, she was confused, unable to figure how to right herself. Her blood pressure rose, lungs ached, and her mind swam with confusion.

No longer able to hold her breath, Jay opened her mouth and water flooded her lungs. Her vision blurred. The grey-blue of her surroundings faded to black.

* * *

WHISPERS. They snaked their way into Jay's subconscious, connecting with her life force, drawing her up through the water. Jay's head burst through the surface of the water, her lungs emptying with a violent cough as she sucked in air.

She saw Cassie power towards the edge of the pool where Stitch had already pulled himself up onto a rock. She kicked at the water to follow her friends, feeling the rucksack dragging at her back. Cassie reached out from the edge, pulling her up onto the rocks.

'Where's Sammy?' spluttered Jay.

'I take it he can swim?' Cassie said as she looked around the pool then up into the trees atop the white cliffs.

'He can swim.' Something caught Jay's eye on the opposite side of the plunge pool. The grey flint surfaces were darkened, wet, like someone had just climbed out. 'He must be OK.' She pointed. 'In that alcove over there.'

Jay surveyed the water's edge. The water was already still. Above, a clear hole in the undergrowth showed distant sky. The cliff at the top cantilevered a good metre or two out from the edge all the way around, like it had been worn away underneath, scoured by high water levels into the circular, concave neck of a vase. The spots in front of Jay's eyes faded, and she took in the arresting beauty of her surroundings. The ripples through the turquoise blue pool settled so that its surface became static, frozen, reflecting the afternoon sun at its edge. She looked at Stitch. His open-mouthed awe as he looked around. She caught his eye and he shook his head, unable to formulate words.

Cassie called out Sammy's name again, then edged towards the lip of rock to dive in and swim across. Jay held her arm. 'Let's work our way around,' she said, slinging her dripping rucksack back over her shoulders. Stitch brushed his wet hair back and wiped his glasses on his wet top.

The three friends edged around the pool. The water's turquoise sheen lightened further where the sun's rays caught it. Half the pool was in shadow and she guessed there would only be a few hours a day when the sun was high enough for its rays to find their way through the narrow space between the trees at the surface. Birds flapped and fluttered around the chalk cliffs, in homes resting on protruding roots and gathered branches.

From a cave that stretched deep into the cliff, water flowed into the pool, its current visible underwater, some water pouring in from a crevice in the rocks creating a shallow waterfall. The cave's ceiling was too low to walk upright. 'The unnamed river,' Jay said. Cassie looked back at her and then to the mouth of the cave. She dipped her hand into the water, cupping it, allowing it to spill from her fingers. It sparkled as it ran through her hands, as if she were holding diamonds. The scent in the breeze was sweet and fresh. Behind Jay, Stitch stepped over the little waterfall and they pressed on towards the next opening.

The dark patches on the rocks were as Jay had thought, wet from someone dragging themselves from the pool. The alcove that she'd seen from the opposite bank was in fact another cave. That one too was a conduit for water entering the pool. The cave had a narrow opening but then opened out to a wider space, perhaps three metres in height with a river's worth of water flowing in a trough beside a raised section, almost like a canal and towpath. The roar of water echoed around the tunnel, bouncing off the walls and creating a whirling wall of sound.

'Sammy.' Cassie lurched towards the prone figure of Sammy, on the rocks next to the river. Jay hurried after her, a hole in the pit of her stomach.

'He's OK,' said Cassie. 'He's breathing fine. Probably the temperature of the water shocked him more than anything else. Can't see any broken bones or any other obvious damage. He'll come around.'

'How did he get out?' said Stitch.

Sammy stirred. He groaned and moved to sit up, insisting that he was OK but wincing as he moved his left foot. He held his ankle, pulling up his trouser leg to reveal a deep, bleeding gash and swelling. He looked groggy and confused.

Deeper into the cave the thundering river powered past them and into the pool. Jay inspected her brother's ankle. He insisted it was just a sprain. Cassie helped Jay to lift Sammy to a standing position, careful to support his weight. 'How do you break an ankle landing in water?' Cassie said, gently.

'It's not broken,' Sammy said, wincing once more as he tried to put weight on it.

'Let us take your weight,' said Jay. Cassie dragged Sammy's arm around her neck and between her and Jay they helped Sammy further into the tunnel. 'There,' said Jay, nodding towards an opening in the side wall through which they could see light.

They entered a vast cavern, perhaps twenty feet across, with a number of smaller caves leading away from a central atrium. In the roof of the main cavern a shaft rose to the surface, the twilight leaking down to where they stood in the bowels of the hill.

'The Caverns,' said Cassie, her jaw dropping open and a smile forming on her lips.

'The gateway,' said Jay as they lowered Sammy onto a rock.

Before them stood a makeshift kitchen with an open fire pit beneath the shaft that served as a chimney for smoke. It was topped with wood with a grate over as if ready for cooking. To the side were a range of pots and pans of different sizes, all well-used, blackened on the bases and scratched and dented on their sides.

'Someone lives here,' said Stitch.

'Not recently,' said Cassie, lifting the pans one at a time.

She scraped a layer of dust and debris from a saucepan. She picked up and shook an old box of matches, then took one out, striking it against the side of the box. It sparked to life, and she shook it to extinguish the flame.

Jay helped Sammy change his clothes for a dry set he'd stored in a bag in his rucksack. He was in pain, woozy, almost sleepy. 'You OK?' she asked. Sammy nodded, then leaned back against the wall of the cave and motioned his permission for Jay to go and explore.

Stitch was sifting through dust-covered notebooks and papers on a makeshift set of shelves on the opposite wall. He flicked through the pages like they were valuable artefacts, his eyes wide at the wonder of what they had found.

Cassie cleaned up a pan and filled it with water from a source that came through from the rocks.

'It's a solution feature,' Stitch said, looking around the cavern. 'They are quite common, but this one is something else.' Jay frowned at Stitch, not entirely sure what he was talking about. 'Limestone and chalk,' Stitch said. 'It weathers, dissolves in the ground water, sometimes opening up these kinds of underground spaces. You'd normally expect them to collapse in on themselves but this one's intact. I guess there's not much up above, so the ground loads are relatively small.'

Jay's gaze lingered on her friend for a moment, sharing in his wonder. She looked around at the crypt-like structure, with natural arches leading to five or six different underground rooms off the central space. The main cavern itself was like an architectural marvel, a grand design created by the natural world.

'Come by the fire, dry off,' said Cassie as the flames grew around the pan of water, the crackling firewood tinder dry and eager to burn. Jay helped Sammy over to a rock by the fire and the four of them sat and offloaded their bags. Jay took a breath, unable to shake the sensation of being in a dream.

Cassie and Stitch each rifled through their bags, salvaging what they could of the food. Jay opened out the map to dry and pulled out her dad's notebook, protected from the water in its plastic bag. Cassie retrieved the keys to the car and was visibly relieved.

Everything Jay could see looked like it had been made from natural materials, or salvaged. It was clear to her that this was Cassie's grandad's "front of house" as Reuben had called it.

'Bears more than just a resemblance to Dad's stories, eh Sammy?'

Sammy nodded, then grimaced as he lifted his leg to rest his foot up on a rock. Cassie sighed. 'Can you believe it?' she said. 'All this time and it was here.' She looked at Jay. 'My grandad was here?'

Jay nodded. 'You think this is his stuff?'

'Maybe. But it's not been used for years so if he came here like you said, when he disappeared, then he didn't stop for long.'

'Must have gone through,' said Jay.

'You want tea, Sammy?' Cassie said, pulling the pan of boiling water off the fire and onto the side where she'd lined up tin mugs from her backpack.

Jay brought a wad of papers and a notebook from the shelves of the cave and sat next to Sammy. She gave the notebook to her brother and opened out the map on the floor. It was hand-drawn, showing the three rivers converging at a point, and one river flowing out to the south. It was a carefully, intricately detailed map of their location. There were different colours to represent different features.

Even trees were carefully positioned and detailed. The map only extended to a hundred metres or so from the pool, with no details of what lay beyond in any direction, and no indication of an entrance to any kind of underground world beyond the pool.

Sammy closed the notebook and leaned back, closing his eyes. He breathed uncomfortably through the pain in his ankle. Jay looked again at the swelling and the cut. She stood and retrieved a pan, filled it with cold water from the spring and returned to Sammy. She placed the pan under his foot and scooped the cool water on to his ankle from her hands. He sucked in air, straightening and tensing with the pain at first, then relaxing.

'I counted two river connections out there,' said Jay. 'Both incoming. Don't know where the outgoing one is, must be under the surface.'

'Three,' said Stitch. 'The third incoming was that opening a little way up the cliff. About ten feet up.'

'I saw that,' said Jay. 'You think that's the Rother? It was only a trickle of water.'

'I know. It's blocked up somewhere by the looks of it.'

'Did you see the unnamed river?' said Sammy. Jay nodded as she continued to scoop water onto his ankle. 'And?' said Sammy.

Jay paused. 'It was just like Dad described it. Magical.' The cut on Sammy's ankle looked deep and the swelling had grown. They'd never be able to get him out of the pool if he couldn't walk.

'Real enough then,' said Sammy, his gaze drifting around the cavern. 'You think dad's hobbits lived down here?'

She looked around. 'Someone certainly did.'

'What about the gateway?' he said.

'That's what we need to find.' Jay filled her brother in about the visit from Reuben, his encouragement, and the information about Cassie's grandad. Sammy seemed a little shell-shocked. She smiled at him. 'Hey, it's a good thing, it means that Dad was right, there really is something down here.'

Stitch reached out for the notebook that Jay had taken from the shelf. 'Can I see?'

'Look,' Jay said, drawing his attention to the hand-drawn map. 'I think we are in here.' She pointed to the map at a point where a series of connected caverns were sketched. 'That river out there, with the towpaths, that's the Arun like we thought. And the one over on the west side, the cave opening up the cliff, that's the Rother, like you said. The third one, on the east side, is the unnamed one, comes down from the north.'

Jay felt a shadow of fear pass across her as she thought of Dad on his own on the run, trying to find his way to the gateway. 'He talked so much about this place but we just thought it was all in his head. The fact that he'd made it all up was part of the magic.'

'But we aren't safe yet. I don't think *this* place is protected. This is not the Interland.'

Cassie called them over from across the other side of the cavern. Stitch and Jay joined her at the shelves. She pointed at one of the maps with hand-written annotations. 'This is my grandad's writing, I'd recognise it anywhere.' The three of them read the words for a minute, seeing that Cassie's grandad had made notes about the various caves and caverns as if he had been systematically exploring and mapping.

'You think he was looking for the gateway?' said Stitch.

Cassie looked at Jay. 'Jay had a visitor last night, a

Runner from the Interland.' She turned back to the shelves, leaving Jay to explain it to Stitch.

Stitch became agitated. 'We don't have time to wait. If the Readers are on their way here, we need to keep going.'

'It's been hidden for a reason, we aren't likely to find it easily. We should rest, then work carefully through the clues they've left for us.'

Sammy looked up. 'And Dad's on his way, can you feel him?'

Jay shook her head. Stitch settled by the fire with one of the notebooks that Cassie had identified as one of her grandad's diaries. Jay put a hand on Cassie's arm.

'I'm OK,' she said, pulling away and avoiding Jay's eye. Jay walked away, taking a seat with Sammy and Stitch.

Stitch pulled a book from his bag, checking it had remained dry. He flicked through the pages.

'What is it?' asked Jay.

'Something I got from the pagans up on Highdown,' said Stitch, squinting through his glasses in the dim light.

'You never said...'

Stitch looked up and smiled at Jay. 'They reckon I might have some power.'

Jay laughed, then felt bad for belittling the possibility of power in her friend. She too sensed that Stitch had something, and Reuben had implied the same. 'Sorry, didn't mean to laugh,' she said. 'What's the book?'

'Healing,' said Stitch. 'It's about the theories of connection, the healing potential of the powers.'

'You think there's something in it?'

'Probably not,' said Stitch.

Jay reached for the Sasha Colden book and opened it at her bookmark. The light from above had faded, so she leaned in to the light from the fire. The words flowed into her and she opened her mind. It was if she were reading from within the book, from the inside out. She allowed herself to be drawn into the story, the feel of it and the depth beneath the words. She had a sense of connectedness with her surroundings – the air, the rivers, and the energy in all that was living. It was as if her understanding was crystallising despite having no means to articulate it – it was undeniable.

'I get a sense that this gateway needs to be uncovered in some way, activated. It can't simply be stumbled upon and walked through.'

'How do we open it?' Stitch asked.

'I don't know yet, but I suspect that it's in the legend. Must be something to do with the unnamed river.'

'Can we wade upstream?' said Cassie.

Jay shook her head. 'No chance. Too strong to walk against. Perhaps we need to navigate *down*stream, *into* the pool, somehow.'

* * *

STITCH LOADED THE FIRE, its smoke rising up through the shaft to the surface. It grew dark and Sammy slept, his body recovering from the trauma of his injury. Cassie had devoured three of her grandad's diaries. They passed around the bottle of Dr Pepper and ate the remains of the food they'd picked up at the petrol station. Cassie closed a diary and placed it on the floor in front of her. 'Well, you live and learn,' she said.

'What?' said Stitch.

'These diaries go back to when my grandad was in his twenties. His *twenties*. That's like, more than forty years ago. He'd been coming here since before that, since he was a kid.

He used to fish down here with his mate. They found this place, kept it secret.'

'You are kidding,' said Stitch. 'Why didn't he ever bring you?'

Cassie shrugged. 'His parents, my great grandparents, were working at Amberley House. His mum managed the laundry and his dad was one of the grounds staff. He'd told me that before. I'd visited the place with him. They came to England from the Caribbean, after the war. He came over with his mum, a few years after his dad travelled here to find work. Why did he never tell me he knew where this place was?'

'I reckon he was going to,' said Jay. 'But this was his place, he was essentially its custodian, protecting the gateway. It was probably his solace. For him and his friend. Does it say what his friend's name was?'

'Pete,' said Cassie.

Jay laughed. 'That's the name of one of the hobbits in Dad's stories, and the other one was Jack.'

'My grandad.' Cassie grinned. 'My grandad's name is Jack.'

'Reuben said your grandad has power,' said Jay.

'It doesn't surprise me. It's Reuben's power that surprises me most. Level seven is serious. I'd have noticed something.' Cassie drew back her own sleeve and quickly pulled it back down, no sign of any mark. 'What did he look like?'

'Tall,' said Jay.

'He always was tall.'

'Chunky. Athletic I mean. Big hair,' said Jay.

'He still have dreads?'

'More like an afro.'

'According to these diaries, there's a way in and out that

they used,' Cassie said. 'An easier route than the one we took.'

'Where?' said Jay.

'They used to come in via the Arun, on a raft. The way out is under the water in the pool.' Jay looked over at Stitch and he nodded.

'Everything's connected,' said Jay.

Cassie said, 'The last diary entry is from around the time he went missing, when he went through, like Reuben said.'

28

The Readers drove as deep into the woods as their Land Rover would take them, before ditching it to continue on foot. Marcus worked on intuition, pulling himself towards the girl by the trail of crumbs she'd left behind, and with his sense of connection with the boy. They remained some distance away, he knew that, but they were heading in the right direction, and they were getting closer with every step.

The girl and her friends had stopped. They were no longer moving away from him and he figured they'd reached their destination. More than the girl's magnetic power, the boy drew his attention. He felt something he couldn't yet untangle. It was the boy who sent him the strongest signal.

'Why do we have to walk through this shit, we have the Land Rover, we can go around,' said Jimmy, sharpening a length of willow to spike and smoke the fish Marcus had pulled from the water.

'This is the only way,' Marcus said.

On his last check-in with the authorities he'd been

informed of Ben's escape from prison. Marcus was the one who had located Ben, for Jimmy to bring him in, so he took the escape as a personal slight.

'He's out, isn't he,' said Drake, a nervous wobble in his voice which Marcus took to be an apology for reading him without asking.

Marcus nodded. 'If I'm reading it right, he's on his way to the girl, so we should be reunited with him before long, and Jimmy can have another go at him, eh Jimmy?'

'Who?'

'The girl's father. He's out, and he's with another one of them, a level two or three.'

'They'll be no bother,' said Drake. Marcus figured that the other Readers would be heading in from different routes to converge at the location of the gateway. They'd not be far behind, but it was possible they'd arrive after Ben. The girl and her friends would stand no chance of escape against the full force of the State. She might put up a resistance against Marcus, but it would be nothing in the face of multiple Readers. If they responded as he'd instructed, there could be six Readers, most at level six or seven. He couldn't afford to be careless. He'd do it right this time.

29

J ay's mind raced. She opened her eyes to focus on something static to stop the cavern spinning.

Shivering in the cool, damp air, she stood and pulled up the hood of her top. She collected logs from a small store next to the fire pit, fed them into the embers, and soaked up the warmth as orange light flickered and danced across her face.

The fall into the pool brought home the sharp reality of the danger she had put herself and her friends in, not to mention her little brother Sammy. Their arrival at the pool had both raised the stakes and cleared away the mist of uncertainty. She had a goal, and it was clearer to Jay what she needed to do.

She sat by the fire, the heat from the flames on her back. She sucked air deep into her lungs and closed her eyes. There was life and energy in the caverns. Surrounded by the earth on all sides, in the heart of a hill fed by three rivers, Jay could feel the power. She let it come, opening to its whispers.

With the force of the environment flowing through her,

she sensed its urgency, its desire for a connection, not just with her, but with all people. She let herself open and flow with the power all around her. Jay breathed deeply, her eyes closed but seeing more than ever before, feeling more than she was able to understand.

The roar of the river Arun just outside the cave was deafening, louder, rumbling – then nothing. The flames of the fire froze in mid-flicker. Out in the tunnel, the surface of the river was still, like the rough surface of a solidified stream of lava. The whispers buffeting her mind became more subdued. They had her attention now.

Jay felt the substance of her surroundings as if it were in her hands, its texture, the strands of its energy taking an almost physical form. Jay assumed the control. She released the time-freeze, allowing the river to explode into action, the flicker of the fire once more illuminating the entrance to the cave. She breathed in once more and the river slowed to a halt, the surface of the water taking a new shape, the juts and spikes like rough icing on a cake. She released the tension in her body and allowed the water to flow, the fire to burn, and the environment to breathe once more.

She sensed that the power and the energy were with her, there to support her. But there was something else. There was a quid pro quo, a need of the environment in return. She sensed that the answers lay beyond the portal, in the Interland, and the path was becoming clearer.

30

J ay woke, the Sasha Colden book on the floor next to her. She looked over to see that Stitch wasn't there. A flicker of candlelight from an adjacent cave caught her eye.

Chalky gravel stuck to her bare feet as she picked her way over to the entrance to the cave. Stitch saw her as soon as she poked her head around the corner. 'Can't sleep?' he said, returning his attention to a bunch of papers on the grey-white floor. 'Come, sit here.' Stitch motioned to the space next to him. 'See what you can make of these maps, there's something here I just can't piece together.'

He had an old OS map open in front of him, much older than any she'd seen before. He nudged it towards her and she turned it over to see if it had a date, or an edition number. Its front cover was missing. She ran her finger across its pages. Its yellowing surface was smooth to the touch, its text and labels in an unusual font compared to modern maps, and its features less complete, like there were layers of information missing, only the essential elements plotted.

'Looks old,' Jay said.

'There are things here that aren't on our map.' Jay strained her eyes in the gloom of the candlelight to see if she could recognise any landmarks. Stitch switched on his head-torch and passed it to Jay.

'Trace the path of the Arun, up from the coast.'

Jay found Littlehampton, from the shape of the coast, although it was labelled as *Hampton*. The river was labelled as the Arun.

'We have a better map than this,' Jay said.

'From what I read in that old notebook,' said Stitch, 'if it's after nineteen forty, it won't show the truth. Have you found the Arun?'

'Yes.'

'Follow it north. Through Arundel, and into Amberley. See where it crosses the Rother?'

'Yes, just north of Amberley. Roughly where we are.'

Stitch leaned over the map with Jay. 'See there,' he pointed, 'there's a third river to the east. That's the continuation of the Arun. The rivers converge here, and run south together, towards the coast.'

'So where's the third incoming river?' asked Jay.

'There are *three* flows coming into the pool, right, like we saw, and one going out, which we reckon is below the surface. So that's what we see here on this map, except that the third incoming river is not so obvious.'

'Tell me something I don't know,' said Jay.

'See the dotted line stretching to the north?'

'That's a footpath, surely?'

'What colour is it?'

'Grey, same as everything on this map.'

'Look closer, what other features match that colour?'

Jay strained to discern the different shades in the lines

on the map. It took a while to tune her vision, but it was clear that the dotted line to the north was intended to represent the same feature as the rivers marked to the south, west and east. 'It's the same shade as the rivers, but...'

'But it's dotted?' Stitch finished her sentence.

'Yes.'

'So what do you think that means?'

'That it's underground?' Jay said. 'But so are the others and they're not dotted on the map.'

'I think the others are only underground in the immediate vicinity of the pool, they are above ground as soon as they escape this hill – the other one, the unnamed one, is underground, according to that map, for several miles.'

Jay followed the dotted river north on the map until it disappeared. 'It heads up towards the River Wey, according to this map, but the line stops somewhere in the North Downs.' Jay leaned in to see where it disappeared but the map features were so basic there was nothing much to see.

'Remind me what else your dad said about the unnamed river?'

'It's the one you have to navigate into the pool to unlock the magic,' Jay said.

'So, maybe that's why there's nothing obvious here. No portal, no gateway. We need to travel the unnamed river towards the pool, which flows through this hill. Maybe there's something inside the hill, on the path of that river?'

'Or maybe it's a magic spell that gets cast when the stars align and the hobbits do a dance,' Cassie said with a snort. She sat down with a huff, cross-legged on the floor, her long legs nudging up against Jay's.

'Yes, very funny,' Jay said.

'But seriously, why didn't someone else do it? Like my grandad?' Cassie said.

'He could have,' said Stitch. 'Was there anything in his notes about looking for the connection of the unnamed river with the real world rivers?'

Cassie shook her head and Stitch sighed.

'What?' said Jay.

'Something in the legend I keep thinking about,' Stitch said. 'The magic is formed through a connection between the unnamed river and the Given. The sister from the legend. She had powers, right?' Jay nodded. 'So it's *you* that needs to navigate the unnamed river, Jay.'

Jay knew this before Stitch said the words. And she knew that it was to do with the Sasha Colden book. Something in that book was connecting Jay with the power in a way that was unique to her, and Sasha. Jay pulled back her sleeve to look at the number on her wrist. If she had such power, she'd surely be sensing the gateway. She frowned and leaned over the map again. 'The location of the connection is not on this map. And that stretch of underground river, down to the pool, is not on any contemporary maps, nor is it listed in any literature I found in the bookshop.'

Jay bit her bottom lip. 'If we can find that connection we can travel the unnamed river down to the pool.'

'You think it's possible?' Cassie said.

'We can try.' Jay arranged the map on the floor and then leaned back against the wall with Stitch, who had his eyes closed, breathing steadily.

Jay stood, and headed into the main cavern to retrieve the OS map, drying by the fire. Jay could hear the trickle of fresh water through the rocks battling against the roar of the Arun out front. Sammy was motionless, breathing out sleep noises. Jay put a couple more logs on the fire and retraced her steps to the side cave where Cassie continued to study the map and Stitch was fast asleep up against the wall. She motioned at Cassie to follow her back into the main cavern where they spread the two maps alongside each other by the fire.

Together, the girls studied the terrain between the River Wey and the pool. The old map showed most of the underground river as it meandered north from the pool, but not the connection with the Wey. The more detailed map showed the topography of the area as well as geographic features. They could see the peaks and troughs of the Downs, the valleys and the hills.

'Maybe we can predict the path of the underground river all the way through to where it connects with the River Wey. We can compare the river as it was shown on the old map, against the terrain shown on the new map, and maybe get a sense of how it reacted to the topography, how it meandered and how it passed through the land. Then we project that route onto the OS map. What do you think?' Jay said.

'I like it!' Cassie said and they high-fived.

* * *

'STILL CAN'T SLEEP?' Stitch asked, joining Jay a few hours later in the main cavern. Jay smiled at him and continued with her pencil, plotting the last sections of the path of the underground river onto the map.

Jay and Cassie had worked out that there were two possible locations where the connection could be. After Cassie fell asleep, Jay studied the possibilities. The one out east was not likely, given that its path was so tortuous, and the connection with the Wey was in a town centre so not likely to be easily hidden and undiscovered for all this time. The western connection was most likely. It followed the trajectory of the marked section of the river, with a logical path through the valleys of the Downs. It connected with the Wey where it passed through woodland that, like the pool, had no obvious paths or access ways. It looked as if it were only accessible from the river itself. The point of connection was just a few miles west of a place where Jay and Sammy used to go fishing with their dad.

Stitch gave Jay a look, like he was impressed, and squinted to see where she'd predicted the connection to be with the River Wey. 'That's where we need to go,' he said, 'and soon. The Readers must be close.'

31

B en woke with a chill in his bones, wet from the rain and a night of fitful rest. Matchstick had been snoring from the moment they set down. Even still, he slept.

Ben crawled out of their makeshift camp under the bridge by a canal. He stretched and scrambled down the slope from the bridge abutment and onto the path. He still wore his prison-issue clothes, the left knee of his trousers soaked in blood. A dog-walker on the opposite towpath glanced over and Ben turned to shield the man's view from his face. For all he knew, their faces were already on the day's front pages.

He brushed himself down and took a moment to breathe in the freedom and tranquillity of the forest. Over the fence and across a car park was a superstore, raising a pang of hunger in his belly. He scrambled over the fence and made his way through the car park towards the store.

He headed first for the toilets, washing his face and rinsing his hair before taking the time to pick the gravel from his knee and rinse it clean. He pulled off his prison top and tied it around his waist, looking less conspicuous in his tee-shirt.

The shop had more staff than customers, packing shelves and organising tills. He picked a trolley and worked through the store, avoiding shop assistants. He started in the clothing section, choosing a couple of backpacks and then picking out some clothes for himself. He guessed Matchstick's size, erring on the large side. In the pharmacy section, he collected plasters and antiseptic spray. He completed his shop with packets of cheese, cold chicken, two loaves of bread and bottled water, which he put straight into the rucksacks in his trolley.

Ben loitered behind a clothes display, noting the position of the security cameras. He dumped the prison outfit and pulled on the fresh new clothes. He crammed the rest of the gear into the rucksacks and, slinging one over each shoulder, walked calmly to the exit, not stopping until he'd reached the other side of the car park. He jumped over the fence with more vigour than earlier and jogged along the path back towards the bridge.

Matchstick was standing on the path with two men. He caught Ben's eye and shook his head. Ben turned, passed along a stretch of path before ducking behind a bush so that he could watch from safety.

The men had uniforms but weren't police. Ben couldn't sense any powers. Matchstick looked as if he were deep in a negotiation when suddenly the two men laughed, patted Matchstick and turned to leave.

'What the fuck?' Ben said as Matchstick reached him, checking over his shoulder to be sure the two men had gone.

'Security guards from the industrial estate. They wanted to take me in to the shelter.'

'Here, get rid of those prison overalls. I hope these fit.'

'Stylish,' Matchstick said, holding out the top.

Ben turned to the other rucksack and opened a loaf of bread, handing a slice to Matchstick.

When Matchstick had dressed himself and discarded the old clothes in the bush, the men ate, drank and tended their wounds, saying little about the previous night and how close they had come to not making it out. Matchstick's graze on his back was worse than Ben had thought, a scrape from his shoulder bones down to his coccyx. He helped Matchstick clean it up.

'You gonna contact the old lady?' said Matchstick as Ben tended his wound.

Ben shrugged. 'She'd as likely hand us in as help us out. What about you? Anyone to contact?'

'Nope.'

Ben looked into the sky, noting the location of the sun to get his bearings. He could see that the canal ran east-west as he'd hoped, which meant that it was the Wey & Arun Canal that he'd intended they find and head west. On foot, it could be three days' walking before they needed to diverge from the river and head into open country. If they could find themselves a boat, they would be there in less than twenty-four hours.

'That way?' asked Matchstick, pulling on his top and looking west, reading Ben's mind.

Ben nodded and stood, stretching. 'Could do with a boat.'

Matchstick motioned downstream where Ben could see narrowboats moored along the canal's edge. 'You know how to drive one of those?' asked Ben.

'Born and bred on the London waterways, my friend. Lead the way.'

32

The sun was high in the sky, its rays penetrating deep into the surface of the pool. With a bird's-eye view, you might easily miss the opening through the trees to the pool below, a mere glimmer of cobalt in an otherwise emerald carpet, the rivers converging on the hill like pulmonary routes to a heart.

Sammy's ankle was no better in the morning. Jay strapped it up, then, with Cassie, helped him outside the cavern to sit by the edge of the water in the pool, at the base of the chalk well that had been their entrance the previous day. Jay was anxious to get moving but couldn't consider leaving Sammy.

They picked their way across the rocks, edging towards the unnamed river connection where the green-blue water quietly pushed its way into the pool, creating streamlines and eddies in the darker blue-grey of the pool. The water forced its way through the connection with a power that was too great to battle against, confirming Jay's thought that they'd not be able to work their way upstream.

Jay sat next to Sammy on a smooth rock and leaned back

against the vertical white face of the cliff that stretched up and into the greenery. The trees soared, making way for a circular patch of cloudless blue sky. Cassie snorted a laugh. 'Look at that cliff. Our fall could have been nasty. *Should* have been nasty. Good chance of smacking into the rocks on the way down.'

'Best not think about it.' Jay grimaced. It was like being at the bottom of a well, twenty metres across at its base and rising fifty metres in white chalk, then a further fifty in the trunks and branches of the trees. She dipped her hand in the flow of the unnamed river, icy cold on her fingers and clear as tap water as it escaped her grasp and continued into the pool. A sweet smell of nettles came in with a breeze and filled the cave.

'You need to leave,' said Sammy.

Stitch emerged from the main cavern with a notebook in his hand and made his way around the pool to take a place on the rock next to Sammy. He shifted around, looking over towards the river connection in the cliff-side.

'What's up, Stitch?' said Jay.

'Not sure yet,' he said, opening the notebook. 'You know that opening up there, the Rother connection that we were talking about?' He nodded up to the cave opening that they had figured was where the River Rother connected to the pool, only a trickle of water coming through.

'What about it?' said Jay.

'There's a reason it's just a trickle.' Jay, Sammy and Cassie waited for Stitch to elaborate. 'There's a natural blockage, according to these notes. Your grandad's notes I guess, Cassie?'

Cassie leaned over to look at the handwriting. 'Looks like it. Old notes though.'

'It takes exactly twenty-four hours for a pressure to build

up. It seems that it's partly due to the natural rising water levels in the ground behind the rock face, with time, and then there's a tidal element.'

'Tidal? Here?' said Jay.

'Yes, the location of the moon and all that, pulling and dragging the ground water. The combination of the tidal cycles and the pressure build-up creates a periodic release.'

'What kind of release?' said Jay, looking up at the hole in the side of the cliff.

'A big one,' said Stitch. 'These notes say that after a release, the rocks, chalk and sandy deposits re-form within the opening, a few tens of metres back into the cliff face, blocking it up again.'

'How did they know that?' said Sammy.

'Because it all comes out in a massive blow out. Then the ground fills back in and it starts all over again. And, because, according to the notes here, it happens every twenty-four hours. Like clockwork.'

'When?' said Jay.

'Some time in the afternoon. So let's watch.' Cassie and Jay looked at each other and then to Stitch, who looked up at the gentle trickle of water from the Rother. Stitch gave Jay a half smile before resting his head back on the white cliff, looking up into the trees. 'See there, about halfway up the cliff?'

'Uh huh,' Jay said, squinting to see a bird resting on a protruding tree root, looking down on them. 'The Phoenix,' Jay said under her breath.

'Like your dad said.'

'My grandad talked about a bird,' said Cassie. 'Said that it used to come to him. What is it?'

'It's a falcon,' said Stitch, 'see the yellow colouring around the eyes and beak, and the claws. It's a female.' He turned to Jay. 'Have you tried to see where your dad is? He could be here?'

'He's not here,' Jay said. 'We need to get back to the car.'

'We know the way out,' said Cassie, standing and looking into the pool for signs of the underwater connection. She looked up towards the falcon. It was restless, moving along the branch and back again.

'What's up with her?' said Stitch.

'She wants to come,' said Sammy. 'Cassie, hold your arm out, she wants to come to you.'

'No way,' said Cassie, but at the same time raising her right arm in front of her. 'She'll never come.' The falcon watched, gave a squawk. Cassie lowered her arm and turned back to the others. 'Look at her. She thinks I'm an idiot, she's laughing at me.' The falcon continued to jiggle on the branch, flapping and nudging along. She squawked again and seemed to topple from the branch. She pumped her wings and soared up towards the trees.

'If she would go to Grandad...' Cassie stretched out her arm. The bird disappeared into the trees. Suddenly, she appeared in the middle of the circle of blue, diving like an arrow towards them. Stitch squeaked in alarm but Cassie stood firm, her arm outstretched. The falcon swooped and opened its wings, slowing almost to a stop in mid-air just above Cassie, then gracefully landing on Cassie's shoulder, ignoring the outstretched arm. Cassie had to bite her lip not to scream out as the falcon's talons gripped the skin of her shoulder.

Jay's mouth hung open with surprise.

Cassie's grin filled her face as the stunning creature settled on her shoulder, her friends aghast. The falcon seemed to be looking right into Cassie's eyes.

With no warning, the falcon took off again, back towards

the perch. The force as the bird launched was enough to push Cassie back into the cliff face, but not enough to wipe the grin from her face as she sat back down next to Jay.

'Wow,' said Jay. Cassie rubbed her shoulder, leaning back and squinting up at the sky through the circular gap in the trees.

'When are we getting out of here?' said Stitch.

Cassie again looked into the pool. 'If the notebook is right, this leads down into the village.'

'So we have to go down there?' said Stitch.

'Definitely,' Cassie said. She stripped off her top and shorts and slipped into the water, bobbing up to the surface and squealing with the cold. She took a deep breath and disappeared. Jay looked at Sammy and Stitch who both stared as Cassie broke the surface and gulped in some air.

'It's there,' she said. 'Less than three feet down, an opening that slopes down through the rocks.' She pulled herself out of the water and Jay noticed Sammy averting his eyes. 'If the notebook is right, at the end of that tunnel, you get to a shallow waterfall…'

'Waterfall?' blurted Jay.

'A little one, a gentle hump that you pass over. Then it's a leisurely drift down for a mile or so and you're in the village.'

'With our rucksacks?' said Jay.

'We could leave them here, we're coming back, remember?'

Stitch stood up next to Cassie, handing her a top to drape over her shoulders. 'We can take a few bits in the small rucksacks, in plastic bags to keep it dry,' he said.

'This is the only way out.' As Cassie spoke, Jay felt the ground begin to vibrate, a low rumble passing up through her body. She looked at Stitch, then over to the cave connection.

'We need to move,' said Stitch, reaching out a hand for Sammy. The rumbling increased in volume and the four moved with more urgency.

Jay and Cassie reached the cover of the opening to the main cavern. They looked back to see a burst of debris shoot across the pit and hammer into the opposite white cliff face like bullets from a gun. Debris rained down on Stitch as he shoved Sammy to safety, stumbling and almost losing his footing on his bad ankle as Jay caught his arm. Stitch followed, soaked and battered. The stream of water that followed the debris must have been more than two metres in diameter, exploding from the entrance of the cave. It powered across the pool like a jet-washer, dislodging chunks of chalk from the cliff as they watched.

After less than a minute, the jet abated, and the flow reduced back to that of a gentle waterfall into the pool.

I don't think I'll be coming with you for this bit,' Sammy said.

'Rubbish. You'll be fine. We can help you,' Jay said as she and Stitch organised the rucksack they'd take underwater.

'The water might be OK but what then? I can't walk on this. You'll be hours with me in tow.'

Jay looked out over the pool, a ripple on the surface as a fish came up for a gulp of air, or an attempt to take one of the pond skaters that skimmed the surface. Her mind returned to her efforts with her powers in the night, the control she felt over time, her environment, the power of the river. 'You know I told you about that weird time freeze thing that happened back at the café?'

'Has it happened again?'

'I might be able to show you.' She closed her eyes and the whispers came –urgent, rushed, more desperate than before. Within a few seconds, Jay had control. She opened her eyes, exhaled and maintained the freeze. She looked up into the sky, a bird frozen in flight. She turned to Sammy – frozen. Closing her eyes once more, she took a breath and put a hand on Sammy's arm, releasing him. He sucked in a breath and coughed as if coming up for air. He jerked his head to look at Jay. 'What the...'

'It's OK,' said Jay.

'What happened? Why has it gone so quiet?'

'Look at that bird,' she said, nodding into the sky.

'What the...' Sammy said again.

'And look at the surface of the water, the insects and the pond skaters.'

'It's frozen,' he said.

'Exactly.'

'Is *everything* frozen?'

'I think so.'

Sammy grinned, then rubbed his eyes, 'Shit, Jay. This is big. You can do anything. We can just walk into a bank and...'

'Sammy,' Jay interrupted. They laughed. 'This is bigger than bank robbery. I feel in complete control, and it doesn't hurt, doesn't wear me down, just feels natural. I wasn't sure if I could bring you in.'

Sammy struggled to his feet and limped over to the edge of the water. He touched his foot on the surface and felt that it was solid, then stepped out onto the flat, silvery surface. Tentatively, as if walking on ice, he moved away from the edge. He laughed, then called for Cassie and Stitch.

'They're not with us,' said Jay.

'Can you unfreeze them?'

'I don't know, I think so. Not now though, we need to go.'

Feeling confident, Jay focused energy on the area of the pool beneath Sammy's feet. It swirled around him as if it were about to become a whirlpool. Sammy squealed, his body turning with the water – once, twice, three revolutions, his scream rising in pitch. She stopped. The surface of the pool steadied and returned Sammy to rest, facing towards Jay.

'This is crazy,' he said.

'Come off the water so I can release it,' said Jay. Sammy edged towards her and she held out a hand. 'There's something in the whispers...'

'Whispers?' Sammy asked as he limped back onto the rocks.

'I get whispers when I connect with the environment. Not intelligible whispers, in terms of their language, but messages that are clear enough to me in a sense.'

'Saying what?'

'Nothing coherent, something about reciprocity,' said Jay. 'What does that word mean to you?'

'Give and take,' said Sammy. 'But what's that supposed to mean?'

Jay released the freeze and the noise of the world returning was deafening. 'I'm not sure yet, but I get a sense that they need help.'

'They?'

'I mean the environment, the eco-systems. They need something. And, for some reason, they see me as part of it.'

'Wow,' said Sammy under his breath.

'It's got something to do with whatever's on the other side of this gateway we are looking for.' Jay looked at her brother. 'That Runner the other night, on the beach.'

'Reuben?'

'They are paranoid and scared to death about the Readers finding the gateway.'

Jay felt a cool wind and shivered. A wave of energy washed over the place and unsettled her for a moment. She helped her brother to stand, then took his weight as they made back to the main cavern to join the others.

It was time to go.

34

M arcus pushed through the undergrowth and out into a clearing by the river. The landscape was flat, and the river seemed to have spread, widening into a lake across a flood plain.

They were close. He'd been searching for the Gateway for years and now he had himself a little homing device, something to draw him in. In all of his previous attempts to complete his mission to weed out the remaining Given, he had failed. It was like trying to find a needle in a haystack. Not this time. This time the needle was calling out to him and he was drawing himself to it like a magnet.

He stepped close to the edge of the water, peering down-stream through the mist. In the distance, in the path of the meandering river, a hill peppered with trees rose out of the ground like a monolith. 'That's it,' he said as Drake and Jimmy pushed themselves through the bushes and into the clearing.

'That mountain?' said Drake, moving to join his leader. 'Couple of hours' walk then.'

'Less, if you two move a bit quicker,' Marcus said

without humour. Jimmy reached down to the edge of the river and took some water into his hands, drinking greedily, then filled his water bottle. Marcus spat into the river.

Jimmy stood. 'What do we do when we get there?' he said.

Marcus looked at him. 'We do what you weren't able to do before. We take her in.'

'What about the Interland?' said Drake. 'If there's a gateway then we need to find it.'

Jimmy snorted. 'The myth? That place was invented by *them* to give them something to fight for. The only place that has a load of the Given all in one place is rehab,' he said.

'It's a good job no one is asking you,' said Marcus. 'If it's there, then we'll find it.' As Marcus spoke, he felt a now familiar slowing of the world around them. Not the complete time freeze he had experienced at the café; this was something different. He turned to observe his two colleagues, both moving as if in slow motion – their words still audible. The river flowed but at a fraction of its previous rate, edging over the shallow weir just downstream in a way that appeared non-physical.

'What was that?' Drake said, shaking his head as if trying to empty his ears of water.

'Did you feel something?' said Marcus.

'No,' said Jimmy at the same time as Drake nodded. 'No,' repeated Jimmy. 'What's going on?'

'Something hit me,' Drake said. 'Then you went all weird,' he said to Marcus.

Marcus looked downstream, the river behaving normally again. He had no idea what these time freezes were, but he knew it was to do with the girl. 'Let's move,' he said. 'We don't have much time left.'

35

S ammy sat with Jay as she chose a few necessary supplies and transferred them to the smaller rucksack. She included her change of clothes and sealed everything inside a plastic bag before squeezing it into the rucksack.

Cassie and Stitch were going through the same process using the other small rucksack. She could see that they were arguing over what to take, Cassie wanting to travel light but Stitch choosing to squeeze in as much as they could carry.

'When you get through,' said Sammy, 'open the plastic bag and let it fill with air. Then you can seal it again and use it as a float.'

'I will. Don't worry. I just need you to worry about you. Make sure you keep a lookout for anything unusual. If anything happens, get in the pool and go.'

Jay sensed something. She couldn't pin it down as a Reader. It felt more like a weak Scanner, but she couldn't be sure, what with the waves of power coming through from all around. Either way, if there were any Readers or Scanners close by, that was bad news. 'Sammy, why don't you rest out by the pool where you can get a view of all the connections, just to be safe?'

'I will, Jay. Until that Rother connection goes again.'

'Yeah, you might want to avoid that.'

Jay called over to Cassie, 'How far down is the opening?'

'A few feet, you'll be fine. We'll be in the village before you know it.' Jay liked to think that she wasn't worried about going through an underwater tunnel with no certainty of its length or whether it led to the open air or hit a dead-end in the side of the hill, but she was struggling to convince herself.

'Just follow me, Jay, keep close,' said Cassie.

'Why don't I go first, then you can push me along if I get stuck,' Jay said.

'You sure you don't want me to rig up a rope for you to follow?'

'Would you?' Jay said. 'Have you got a rope?'

Cassie laughed. 'I was joking, Jay. It's a couple of feet down to the opening, we'll be out the other side in one breath.'

THE READERS ENTERED the cave in the side of the hill, their raft bumping up against the rocks at the sides as they edged closer to the pool. Marcus pulled the raft to a stop as they reached the mid-point. Light penetrated only from one end and Jimmy was eager to get back out in the open. It was the noise that was most disturbing, the echo of the sound of the running water reverberating off the rock tunnel walls, like an aeroplane taking off.

Jimmy glanced at Marcus, standing at the helm like a ship's captain. He was miles away, focused on something they couldn't see. Jimmy looked at Drake who shrugged, as if to say that they just needed to let him do what he had to do, whatever that was.

Jimmy looked into the distance as they edged downstream. He could see the turquoise glow of the surface of the river as it emerged into the pool and into sunshine. He was reminded of the lake near his childhood home where he and his brother would go swimming on the weekends. He was drawn to it, impatient to get there.

* * *

JAY HAD JUST DRAGGED the rucksack over her shoulders and tightened the straps when she felt it – a force like a power-drill piercing her temples. This was different to the power she'd experienced when Marcus was close. This was energy targeted directly at her.

Her hands at her temples, Jay squeezed her head to push out whatever was infiltrating her mind. Through blurred vision she saw that Sammy was holding her wrists, speaking to her, terror on his face. She could hear nothing but muffled voices. Cassie was there too, holding her and guiding her to sit. Jay couldn't let go of her head for fear of it exploding with the pressure and pain. Stitch rushed over to her with some water that he poured into his hands and splashed onto her face in a desperate attempt to help.

Jay's dad had told her how the powerful Readers could cause pain and lasting damage. She knew who was responsible for the attack on her mind. Marcus had the power to get inside her head. He was near. He was stamping around in her head. He was relentless. Jay sucked in a breath and screamed as she released it. She took another breath. She concentrated, trying to resist him. Push him away. 'Get out,' she screamed, causing Sammy to release her wrists and Stitch to take a step back. Jay screamed once more, 'Get out!'

Cassie caught Jay as her legs gave way and she slumped onto the floor, conscious but no longer in control of her body. Her mind was becoming the property of another. Her final thought as the fog descended was that they would come now. And there would be nothing to stop them. Jay wouldn't be able to protect her friends or Sammy. She had put them in danger. She had failed.

* * *

'BE PATIENT,' said Drake, reading Jimmy. 'Let him do his thing.'

Jimmy looked quizzically at Drake. 'What's he doing?'

'Digging,' said Drake. Jimmy's frown deepened. Drake elaborated, 'He's digging into her mind, debilitating her. Now that we are close enough.'

'She's mine, remember. I'm the one she gave the slip. I need to bring her in.'

Drake rolled his eyes. 'This isn't about you, Jimmy. Stick to the plan. Marcus does his thing, then we walk in there and take her away.'

Marcus seemed to come around. 'She should be a bit more manageable now.' They picked up speed, shooting towards the mouth of the cave where the River Arun met the magical pool.

* * *

SAMMY TOOK A DEEP BREATH, trying to calm himself, thinking he'd be no use to Jay if he couldn't keep calm. He leaned over her. She was still breathing. He lifted one of her eyelids to see that her eyes had rolled back in her head. 'We need to get her to a hospital.'

'That's not going to happen,' said Cassie. 'There's no way we are getting her through that underwater tunnel if she's unconscious.'

'Then the hospital needs to come here,' Sammy said, eyes wide, panic surfacing. He forced himself to take slow and steady breaths. 'How about you go, Cassie? Get to the village and call for help.'

'Where do we tell them to come to? Where does the ambulance go?'

'They can get a chopper in here,' said Stitch. Sammy put his arms under Jay and pulled her up to a sitting position. She stirred and Sammy's heart leaped with hope, relief. 'Jay? Talk to me.'

'They're coming,' she mumbled as she battled to hold herself upright. She flopped to the side and Sammy pushed her back up again. 'Readers.'

Cassie jumped into action. 'We need to leave.' Sammy heard a noise behind them, someone approaching from the direction of the Arun. He looked up at Stitch, then turned to see three men enter the cavern.

'Here we are,' the tallest one said. Sammy could tell by their distinctive outlines that these were the three men from the car park at the café: the short and wide one, the tall and skinny, and the tall and bulky. All were in black. He remained crouched next to Jay. Her eyelids fluttered and opened. She put a hand on Sammy's arm. He looked at Stitch again and then over to where Cassie had been. She'd gone. Melted away into the adjoining caves and Sammy was glad that she was out of reach of the Readers. Stitch stood, taking a position in front of Sammy, a protective stance. He stepped towards the three men.

'What do you want?'

'Her.' The tall and bulky one nodded at Jay as she pushed herself up from the floor, rejecting Sammy's attempt to help her.

Sammy looked to the tall man, their leader, a long scar on the side of his face. Their eyes locked and Sammy knew he was Marcus, the level eight that Jay had talked about. Marcus continued to look Sammy in the eye. Sammy felt the connection strengthen, as if it were more than simply this Reader's need to take them in. Marcus dragged his eyes from Sammy and made towards Jay. Stitch stepped to intervene but Marcus did something to cause him to cry out in pain, his hands squeezing the sides of his head.

'Leave him,' said Sammy.

Marcus looked at Sammy. 'You're the brother,' he said. Sammy nodded and looked sideways at Jay, seeing her straighten and focus on Marcus.

Marcus stopped mid-sentence as Jay raised her hands to the side of her head and Marcus rocked back on his heels before recovering.

'I like your spirit, Jay. Not many would have survived that degree of digging. But you...'

'Leave us alone,' Jay said as Sammy and Stitch stood, both unsteady on their feet. For a moment, a flicker of compassion for Marcus had stirred in Sammy, but it was short-lived. Whatever his connection to this man, his connection to Jay was far more powerful.

'We can't leave you alone. You know that. But I'm sure we can come to an arrangement. We want to know about the gateway.'

'What gateway?' said Jay.

Marcus turned to Drake and smiled. 'The gateway that your old man is on his way here to find. The gateway that you kids came here for. The Interland. We all want the same thing.'

'There is no gateway,' said Jay, and she seemed to push again at Marcus with her mind so that he stumbled back once more, this time clutching his head in the same way that Jay and Stitch had done a few minutes before.

Jay screamed and doubled over, her hands on her head. Marcus stepped up next to Drake, and then Jimmy stepped forward. The three of them focused on Jay and she crumpled, sliding to the floor. Stitch shouted for Marcus to stop but the shorter of the Readers pushed him away, knocking his head on the limestone wall of the cave.

Sammy went to his sister. She showed no sign of understanding that he was there, nothing in her eyes but pain. He turned and rushed at Marcus, stumbling on his damaged ankle and slamming into him with no effect, like hitting a wall.

Everything stopped. Sammy fell on his face in the dust. Stitch struggled to his knees and then slumped back down in the dirt on his front. Sammy turned his head to see Jay. She lay motionless, her eyelids flickering and then opening. She looked at Sammy. Her eyes full of sorrow, pain and fear, not for herself, but for him, and Stitch, and Cassie.

'They don't know,' Marcus said.

'There is no gateway,' said Drake.

'If there is,' Marcus said, crouching down to Jay, 'then these idiots don't know about it. Take those two outside,' he said to Drake. He and Jimmy grabbed Sammy and Stitch and dragged them outside to the pool. Sammy caught Marcus's eye as he was dragged away. Nothing. No compassion. No mercy. A minute later, Marcus appeared outside the cave carrying Jay.

'What is it?' Marcus barked at Stitch, who was gazing

intently at the Rother.

'Yeah, what are you looking at? Is that the gateway?' said Jimmy, shifting from foot to foot. He made Sammy nervous, he was skittish and unpredictable.

Marcus looked towards the opening of the cave above them, the connection with the Rother. 'What's with this cave?' he said. Sammy and Stitch kept quiet. Drake began to climb up to the opening but Marcus stopped him. 'That's not it,' he called to his friend. 'They're scared of that opening. It's not the gateway.'

He turned to Sammy. 'What is it?' he said. Sammy said nothing, using his full concentration to keep his mind clear and empty. Marcus looked down at his ankle. 'Put these two up there,' he said, nodding towards the cave. 'Tie them together, we might still need them.'

'Aren't we taking them in?' said Jimmy.

Marcus shook his head. 'I don't think so.' As he turned his back, Sammy launched himself at him, trying to force him into the water. Marcus moved quickly, more than one step ahead of Sammy. He turned, reaching out to Sammy, holding him on the edge of the pool, then flinging him around and into the chalk rock-face. Sammy hit his head and slid to the floor. Marcus frowned at him for a long moment, then turned away. 'Tie them together,' he said again.

'With what?' complained Jimmy.

Marcus said nothing. He walked away, towards the main cavern.

'What about the girl?' called Jimmy.

'Leave her, she's no danger to anyone now,' said Marcus. The words pushed their way into Sammy's head, through his pain and into his consciousness. He felt far away. He tried to open his eyes but couldn't draw the strength.

The pounding in Stitch's head subsided and he gathered his thoughts. His hands were tied to Sammy's with a leather belt and they were sat back-to back in the cave opening by the Rother. In a matter of hours, a force of water and rock would launch them, and anything else in its way, at the opposite cliff face.

Jay hadn't moved from where Marcus left her when he dumped her body next to the pool. He watched her chest to see if she was breathing, but he couldn't tell. As he straightened, leaning back into Sammy, he felt Sammy list to the side. 'Sammy? What's wrong?'

Sammy's eyes were closed, and he was leaning heavily, pulling Stitch over with him. 'Sammy,' Stitch repeated, louder this time. Sammy's eyes flickered open, and he righted himself, taking the pressure off Stitch. 'Sammy, are you OK?'

'I think so,' Sammy said, and the slur in his voice sent a shiver of worry through Stitch.

'Sammy, you feel hot.'

Silence.

'Talk to me.'

'Huh?' Sammy grunted.

Stitch shook himself to jolt Sammy from his slumber, pushing back into him. 'Sammy!'

'I'm OK,' Sammy said, sounding a little more lucid. 'I think I have a fever.'

'You're like a hot water bottle back there.' Stitch turned to see Sammy edge up his trouser leg with his other foot. The entire lower leg was swollen, red and purple with bruising. But more than that, the ankle joint was a deep purple-black colour with yellow pushing through. 'Looks infected,' Stitch said.

'I'll live,' said Sammy.

'You better.'

'Where are Cassie and Jay?' said Sammy.

Stitch hesitated. He nodded in the direction of the pool. 'Jay's down there, she's not looking good.'

Sammy stretched to see his sister, lying next to the edge of the pool. 'I need to get to her.'

'You're not going anywhere,' said Stitch. 'Cassie ducked into the caves when those Readers turned up. She's our best chance.' Stitch looked down at Jay, her face turned towards the water, chalk from the floor in her hair and on her cheek. He pleaded for her to come to, sending messages to her, messages that she'd ordinarily hear without effort. She made no move, no flicker of an eyelid or twitch of a limb.

'Where are the Readers?' asked Sammy.

'In the cavern. They're trying to figure out where the gateway is,' Stitch said, wondering what might happen if Cassie took them on. If there were no powers involved, she'd take all three of them without breaking a sweat, but the odds were against her. Marcus had shown what he could do, even to Jay.

* * *

JIMMY THREW a wad of papers and maps onto the floor, losing his cool. 'This is all shit, nothing useful here.'

Marcus continued flicking through a notebook, occasionally checking something on the map to his side. 'Pick that up, Jimmy.'

Jimmy started to complain but a mere glance from Marcus focused his mind and he re-stacked the maps and papers. 'Where's Drake?'

'Checking through those caves.'

'I thought you said there was nothing down there?'

'We need to be sure,' Marcus snapped. 'There may just be three of them but you talked of a fourth at the house. Another girl?'

Jimmy nodded. 'She's not here.'

Marcus couldn't shake a sense that she *was* there but had slipped away unnoticed.

The notebooks gave him very little. From what he could see, there were no references to a gateway, and he was beginning to think he'd been right, that there was no such gateway, merely a myth to keep up the morale of the Given.

'Hey, Marcus,' Jimmy said. 'What about the father? Is he close?'

'He's on his way. We'll be ready.'

Marcus had gone too far with Jay. He'd been afraid. The girl had power of a sort he'd not seen before, so he had pushed far enough to neutralise the threat. It was reasonable force, he assured himself. He would be questioned back at base. Jay was valuable, someone whose head the authorities would like to get inside. He could get in a lot of trouble for what he'd done to her.

Marcus shook off the thought, re-directing his energy towards his primary goal. The mere presence of the Given threatened his existence. Those with the original power, especially where the power was strong, like in Jay, had the key to neutralising the Readers. Marcus knew that with enough focus, and enough of a coalition of the Given, he could be reduced to less than he was even before his own transformation to Reader. And that was not something he could afford to let happen, not something that this girl would make happen. He would not be stopped from wiping away all traces of the Given, wherever they came from.

'Come with me,' Marcus said to Jimmy, replacing the notebook on the shelf and making his way back outside to the pool. Jimmy followed.

Outside, Stitch and Sammy watched from their elevated position in the cave as Marcus and Jimmy approached. Marcus could sense how unwell Sammy had become. The boy filled him with self-loathing for his own weakness, which turned to anger. He approached the prone body of Jay and looked up at Stitch and Sammy. 'Has she moved?' Stitch shook his head. Jimmy tapped at Jay's body with his foot as if she were a dead animal. He trod on her hand, pushing down so that her fingers squashed into the rock. She made no sound.

'Leave her,' shouted Stitch.

Marcus laughed. 'What's the matter, little Stitch?' With his foot, Marcus pushed Jay over onto her front, her arms twisted beneath her at grotesque angles. Stitch looked away. Sammy's head lolled like it was too heavy for him to keep it up.

Marcus dug the toe of his boot into Jay's side and flipped

her once more. She slipped over the edge of the rocks and into the water. Stitch howled, the sound primal like an animal in pain. Sammy was silent, slumped on his side. Jay made no sound as her head bounced against a rock and she disappeared beneath the surface of the water.

PART V

THE GATEWAY

37

Unconscious, Jay drew a breath, water filling her lungs. Her body shut down, as if giving up the effort to survive. Her lungs made no attempt to eject the water, her temperature plummeted and her organs began to fail.

Her body sank to ten metres below the surface, into a darker, cooler zone. Her body temperature continued to drop until it equalised with the water, dropping from its normal thirty-two degrees to just over nine Celsius, her skin grey like flint.

She took a breath.

Her lungs ejected water and then re-filled as she took another breath. Inside Jay's lungs, something strange was happening. The alveoli became engorged. Her body's reaction to its surroundings was to force the blood flow through her lungs to maximise the oxygen exchange from the water. With this, much like a fish does as it draws water into its mouth, through its body and out through its gills, Jay was able to retain enough oxygen for her reduced body temperature and reduced heart rate to feed her vital organs.

Four minutes after entering the water, Jay had reached a depth of fifteen metres. The temperature of the water had decreased to less than eight degrees. Fish came. They nudged at Jay's body, exploring.

The whispers came again, pulsing like the pumping of a heart, swirling like eddies in the water, or the rush of wind above the surface. They penetrated her mind with ease, sparking the connections inside. Without opening her eyes, Jay came to awareness. With the water in her lungs, the fish at her side, Jay became closer to the power than ever before.

At six minutes, Jay had risen once more to within a few feet of the surface of the pool, a school of fish nudging and encouraging her body into an upward trajectory, towards the opening of the subaqueous tunnel.

Head first, Jay slipped into the suck of the River Arun, pulled into its irresistible force. Plunging steeply, she was cushioned from the rocks by the swirling energy of the water, the streamlines forcing her through to the outside, away from the confines of the pool. Her head bobbed above the water and she coughed. Her lungs emptied, and she drew a breath of fresh air as she slipped onto her back and floated with the current.

Her body temperature continued to rise, her heart rate returned to normal and her skin regained its colour. She blinked away the fresh river water so that the blue of the sky and white of the clouds came into focus. She shivered, moistened her stiff lips with her tongue and breathed deeply. The fresh scent of the river, the sound of the wind in the branches of the sycamore and beech along the banks, was invigorating.

Tentatively, she kicked her legs, then moved her arms, feeling the ache in muscles not yet pumped with blood. She turned and kicked at the water, taking herself in towards the shore, heading for the shallows beneath the bridge. Jay lay in the water and rested. She remained still for some time before dragging herself up and onto the riverbank.

She stood, shaky and dripping. She walked towards the trees, away from the little parade of shops on the other side of the village green and into cover. She walked through landscape that hardly changed, for beyond the trees were more trees.

At a crossroads in the paths through the woods, Jay slumped onto the floor, drained. Her eyes were closed before she reached the ground.

38

Cassie circled back through the caverns, to the tunnel that carried the River Arun through the hill, a few hundred metres upstream of the pool and her friends.

She slowed as she approached the opening to the main cavern. She could hear two of the Readers arguing amongst themselves. At the opening she stopped, then stepped across the cave's entrance and down the final few metres into the area of the pool where streaks of sunlight penetrated from above.

She stood in an alcove in the cliff wall, out of sight, resting her head against the wall and looking up to the sky as if for inspiration. A loud call filled the air with sound.

The falcon launched. Cassie flinched, shook her head, and at the last moment the bird changed course, flapping its wings to take it into the elevated cave entrance to the Rother.

She saw them then. Sammy and Stitch were slumped on their sides as if shot, back to back and wrists bound. The bird took off again, back to its perch. With a last check towards the opening to the Arun, Cassie ran around the pool to her friends. She jumped to get a hand-hold on the ledge that supported Sammy and Stitch, and pulled herself up. From the darkness of the cave she called, 'Sammy? Stitch?'

Stitch stirred. 'Is that you, Cassie?'

Cassie reached out to him, helping him to sit upright, then turned to Sammy. 'Is he OK?' she asked Stitch.

'Infection in his foot. Check him, is he breathing?'

Cassie reached into her backpack and pulled out a bottle of fresh water, pouring a little into her hands and holding it to Sammy's lips. He remained still, no sign of consciousness. 'He's warm,' said Cassie, running her cool hands across his brow. She dabbed his head and neck with water and moved him into what she hoped was a more comfortable position. 'He's breathing, but we need to get him help.'

'Jay's gone,' said Stitch.

'Gone where?'

'She never came around... and... he pushed her in there.' Stitch nodded towards the pool, unable to speak. Cassie, face grey, stammered, unable to release any coherent words. Stitch continued, 'But she's not dead. I can feel her.'

'So you have powers too now?'

'No, she's sending me messages, it's her power, not mine. Nothing clear, but I know she's alive. She went through the exit, under the water, and down to the village.'

'Do you think she's going to the connection?' said Cassie.

'She must be,' said Stitch. 'But that's miles away, and she's stopped. She's alive, but she's not moving. I think I know where. You need to go there.'

Stitch was worn down to his limits. Cassie reached

behind him and started to untie his hands but he stopped her. 'No. There's no point. We won't make it through the exit. I'm not leaving Sammy here. If you untie us, they'll know you've been here.'

Cassie nodded but continued to loosen the knots, easing the pressure on their hands.

'There's a pathway in the village. It leads from the bridge by the river into the woods. She's there, but I don't know how far along. The last signal I got from her was about twenty minutes ago and weak. Fading.' He paused. 'I just hope she's still OK. I don't know what her state of mind is after Marcus's attack. She may be damaged.'

'I'll find her,' Cassie said. She peeked her head around the edge of the cave. 'What are they doing in there?'

'Still trying to find the gateway?' said Stitch.

'I've been all through those caves.' Cassie pulled off her rucksack and checked that her gear was safely contained inside the plastic bag before slinging it back over her shoulders. She dabbed some more water onto Sammy's lips, fed some to Stitch and placed the bottle into his hand. 'You can pull your hands free now. It's loose enough. I'm going before one of them figures out I'm here.'

'Do you know where the connection is?' said Stitch.

'If Jay was right, it's at that little boathouse on the Wey. I'll find it if I can get to Jay.'

'Impossible for anyone but you, Cassie.' Stitch smiled.

'What about Sammy?'

'I've got him,' said Stitch. 'You need to go.'

Cassie considered the option of taking Stitch and Sammy with her. She'd never be able to get all three of them through the opening before the Readers got to them. Stitch guessed her thoughts. 'It's not worth it,' he said. 'Go before it's too late, just hurry.'

Cassie checked Sammy one more time, kissed his forehead to gauge his temperature. 'He's warm, but not hot.' She touched Stitch on the arm, then lowered herself back down to the edge of the pool. Wasting no time, she slipped into the water and almost without creating a ripple, ducked under and swam from sight.

39

J ay felt nothing physical, no touch on her skin, no pain, no physical sensations except for her sense of smell – the trees, the damp leaves that were her mattress, and the sweet scent of the woodland floor. Her strangled thoughts broke free, one by one. Whispers floated, goaded, coaxed her out from herself to a greater consciousness. The resistance she held to the inevitable weakened. Control, burying, hiding, all gone. The desire for obscurity and safety in concealment evaporated.

Jay allowed the whispers room to manoeuvre and explore. She opened to the energy, the power within the ground, the trees, the water – the energy that resides in everything. Images coalesced from the feelings, like the colours she saw in her dad's thoughts, combined with a raw energy that gave them life. Her mind began to piece itself back together, but in a new form, a more robust and resilient form, a form that whilst open to the power and possibility within her connected world, one which was protected and strong.

As Jay's mind mended, and her consciousness returned, an image came to her. Zadie Lawrence. She was smiling, laughing. She was surrounded by tall trees that reached high into the sky, protective and powerful, elegant and beautiful.

40

As Cassie hovered weightless in the space between the pool and whatever would come next, her cheeks puffed and lungs aching to breathe, a picture of her grandad came to her. His face was clear – the deep laughter lines, the soft brown eyes mottled with amber.

She burst the water's surface. Darkness transformed to light. She twisted herself around as she breached, sucking in a breath as she was swept over a cascading weir and downstream, drifting to where the water flowed clear and still.

The banks grew high with reeds, grasses and trees tall and thin. The slopes were scrappy and muddy, holes for otters, river voles and cray fish. Slipping onto her back, Cassie allowed herself to drift downstream, keeping her nose above the surface.

She pulled herself up onto all fours in the shallows under the bridge, the shiny orange stones digging into her hands and knees, and heaved her water-logged body out of the water to lean up against the bridge pier. Pushing away the urge to sit and rest, she pulled off her rucksack, relieved to see that her plastic bag had done its job. She changed quickly, dragging a pair of jeans up her legs and then stuffing her wet things back into the plastic bag. She clambered up the river bank and onto the green, a well-tended stretch of grass with a cricket square fenced off at its centre.

Across the green at a café where out front were a row of old Vespa mopeds, personalised with motifs and flags. She stepped inside. The café buzzed. A group of bikers had occupied the back half of the place leaving the locals to the front. She looked out again at the row of Vespas, which reminded her of her dad's old moped. She knew that if she picked the right bike, there'd be no need for keys.

She left the café, her rucksack on her back, and went to work on the bike furthest from the door. Within a minute, she had forced the ignition barrel and kick-started its engine. She stepped through to sit and push it off its stand, marvelling at how she'd managed to pick the loudest bike in moped history. With a glance over her shoulder she saw that two of the bikers were already out of the café door and running at her.

She let rip. The Vespa shot forward so fast that she lost control, bumping up the kerb and onto the green. The bike shot from under her and spiralled into a heap on the grass. Cassie sat, stunned for a moment. The bike stalled. She dragged herself off the floor and pulled the bike upright, jumping hard on the kick-start as the two bikers crossed the road. The engine fired and she wheel-spun away. She powered full throttle over the green and towards the path that would lead her into the woods, her bike squealing with the effort, the men's shouts growing distant.

With Stitch's instructions in her head, Cassie guided the bike with its Union Jack paintwork through the opening to the woods, the back wheel sliding out with every turn. She bumped along the uneven surface, raising herself off the seat to keep balance. After a few minutes, the path reached a crossroads where it widened to a clearing with a river running alongside, a tributary of the River Wey. Cassie hid the bike behind a log pile twice her height and dragged off her crash helmet, smoothing down her braided hair and rubbing her forehead where the crash helmet had left a mark. She stepped off, her legs aching, wobbly and numb from the vibration of the little two-stroke engine.

'Where are you?' she said aloud, scanning the perimeter of the clearing. She left the crash helmet on the handlebar of the bike and moved towards where the two paths crossed, as Stitch had directed.

'Here,' Jay's voice from behind her.

Cassie let out a sharp scream before covering her mouth to muffle as Jay pulled Cassie into a hug. 'We were worried about you. How'd you manage to get out of the pool?'

Jay shrugged. 'Not even sure myself. How was Sammy when you left? I'm getting bad feelings from him.'

'Not so good. We need to move, find the connection and get back into the pool. Do you know where your dad is?'

'I think I do,' Jay said, a look of understanding on her face, like she'd discovered something at last. 'He was heading towards the pool but I've set him straight. Set him on a course for the boathouse. We can meet him there.' Jay looked at the Vespa and raised her eyebrows at Cassie.

'Jump on,' said Cassie, collecting the other crash helmet and handing it to Jay. Cassie took the front and Jay slung her leg over the back, holding on to Cassie's waist. She kicked it into action and released the clutch. The bike struggled as Cassie manoeuvred it back onto the path. 'Which way?' Jay nodded for Cassie to take the right-hand arm of the crossroads.

As they bumped out of the woods and onto tarmac, Jay pointed the way, shouting to Cassie to be heard above the noise of the engine, 'Follow the river upstream. It's about ten miles to the boathouse.'

Cassie squinted as she rode, the wind dragging tears from her eyes. The River Wey alongside the road was wide and slow moving between the north and south Downs. Algae had formed on its surface, giving it the appearance of smooth Astroturf in places, with scum forming in the stagnant patches as it meandered.

They emerged from under the trees just south of where Cassie figured the boathouse must be. The road diverged from the path of the river and the bike laboured as the hill steepened. From the top of the ridge they could see down over the valleys on both sides, the river pushing north and west below them. They rested in a layby at a fork in the road for a minute and Cassie checked off the landmarks – Chanctonbury visible to the east, the Cathedral spire in the city centre to the north. She looked out over the ridge. 'Which way?' she said, turning back to look at Jay.

Jay nodded to the left. 'That way. Dad's on his way to the boathouse. He's with someone. Let's go.' Cassie pulled away and down the hill to their left, towards the river.

41

Ben pushed forward on the throttle of the old narrowboat, the engine revving hard as it pushed through warm air coming over the flood plain. He could only hope the Readers had lost their scent, at least for the moment.

Matchstick was below deck. The deep thrum of the boat's diesel engine sent vibrations through Ben's feet. It felt good to breathe the scent of engine fumes and fresh pollen off the fields. But he couldn't relax. Jay and Sammy needed him. They were in trouble, he could feel it.

They scraped their way down river, lurching between the banks of the canal. The boat shed flakes of black paint and spewed clouds of oil-blue exhaust smoke as it slewed and squeezed past the private jetties, punching through the trees.

Matchstick stepped up from below deck, eyes scanning the horizon. He sucked on two roll-ups at the same time, exhaling and handing one to Ben. 'Looks like you've got the hang of it?' Matchstick said.

When they'd taken the boat from its mooring, Matchstick had to work his magic to get it going, twisting wires together as Ben controlled the throttle. When it kicked into life, Matchstick took over and steered the old narrowboat downstream. He showed Ben how to throttle and steer before sinking below deck to rest.

Ben was too wired for sleep. His messages from Jay were sporadic, like messages filtered through static, but he knew she was now north of the pool, at an old boathouse, so he set a new course.

Jay and Sammy were in trouble, this he knew. Not for the first time, he wished he had stronger powers. He checked the dials on the instrument panel: oil pressure looked good, engine temperature high but not in the red. No fuel gauge but there were three, full, diesel containers below deck. He leaned up against the old wood of the cabin and ran his hand over its mottled surface, worn smooth over the decades, almost like soap to the touch. With one hand on the tiller, he guided the narrowboat through a canopy of leaves that dipped to anoint them as they passed. Matchstick, the imprint of a pillow lining on his face, shuffled up to the front of the boat and dangled his legs over the edge.

42

J ay saw the boathouse just at the point the little engine in the Vespa chugged and died. 'We can coast in,' she shouted. She felt a warmth that told her she was close to her dad. He was at the boathouse. The hill took them all the way to the car park.

As they rounded the corner of the old boathouse, a neglected wooden-slatted building in need of paint, Jay's dad stood facing them, his back to the river. His friend, Matchstick, sat on the front of a tatty looking old narrow-boat. He skimmed a stone across the surface of the river and then jumped onto the bank to face Jay and Cassie as they descended the slope to the river's edge.

Jay and her dad embraced as Cassie held out a hand to Matchstick. 'Cassie,' she said.

'Pleased to meet you. And you're Jay.' He turned to Jay and seemed to take a little step back as if shocked.

'What?' Jay's dad said to Matchstick.

'The power took me by surprise a little.'

Jay smiled at her dad, felt the usual deep fondness for him that had evaded her when she had visited him in prison. He emitted a different sense to that from before. Escape from prison brings more than physical freedom. It was as if he'd remembered who he was. Jay reached out to him again, and they hugged a second time. 'I missed you.'

'Good to have you back, Jay.'

'We won't get that thing down the unnamed river,' said Cassie, pointing at the narrowboat. Then, motioning to a row-boat tied up alongside the boathouse, said, 'That's more like it.'

Jay looked at her dad. 'We need to move. Sammy's in trouble.'

'How bad is he?'

Cassie spoke up. 'He's got a fever and an infection. He's unconscious.'

'What's the plan, Jay? Why are we here?' said her dad.

While Cassie prepared the boat, Jay told her dad and Matchstick about the connection with the unnamed river, what they'd found in the notebooks and maps at the pool.

'What's it like? The gateway?' he asked.

'Just like you told it, Dad. Just as sparkly, just as magic.' Ben looked down, still thinking about Sammy. 'We met the Phoenix,' she said.

'Seriously?'

'She's a beauty.'

Jay told her dad about Cassie's grandad, his journey to the gateway. About how he'd been going to the pool since he was a kid.

'Where is he now?'

'We think he's on the other side,' said Jay.

Cassie looked up. 'You really think so?' she said, and Jay nodded.

'A chance of keeping some of this freedom,' Matchstick said, throwing their gear into the back of the rowing boat.

Jay stood to help Cassie and Matchstick push the boat into deeper water. Cassie insisted on taking the oars at the back, always in the driving seat. Matchstick took the second set of oars at the front. Jay and her dad paddled through the shallows and climbed into the central section, taking seats alongside each other.

'Let's find this connection,' said Ben.

43

Smoke rose and escaped through the shaft above Marcus's head as he fed reams of papers onto the fire.

Drake returned from his detailed search of the interconnecting caves, looking for an exit. He stepped up to the fire pit. 'What are you doing?' he asked.

'We can't leave this stuff here. There are years of notes, maps and sketches.' He threw another armful onto the fire and the heat warmed his face.

'There might be something in there about the gateway,' said Drake.

Exactly, thought Marcus without saying so. 'There is no gateway,' he said.

Drake frowned. 'Where's Jimmy?' he asked.

Marcus nodded out towards the pool. 'Watching the two boys, and keeping an eye out for anyone coming in via the river connections.' Marcus felt very little energy coming from Sammy and Stitch. Their life forces were weak. Sammy had been unconscious for some time and Marcus wondered how long until he died. Marcus resolved not to allow the boy to leave the gateway. If he were to pull through, Marcus would finish him off. It was the only way to quash the conflict inside him, the confusion that could cause him to lose focus. He couldn't afford to fail. The other one, Stitch, had been weakened by Marcus's infiltration of his mind. He was no longer a threat.

Jimmy entered the cavern. 'Pretty sure those two are dead, neither of them has moved for the best part of an hour.'

'They're not dead,' said Marcus. 'They're weak, but I can feel them.'

'What do we do?' said Drake.

Marcus looked at him, frowned, and returned to feeding papers into the fire.

Drake continued, 'We need to take them in. Alive.'

'Forget them. The father is our target now.'

'But...' Drake started.

'But nothing. Our job is to bring in the Given.' He paused. 'Jimmy, get back out there and watch the connections. You can't afford to lose another one.'

Jimmy and Drake both filed back outside. Marcus looked after them, then threw the last of the papers onto the fire. He could feel the approach of the other Readers, their signal was strong – they were close. But so too was the father, and his signal had strengthened, making Marcus uneasy. There was an uncertainty in the air that he couldn't shift, or make sense of.

44

J ay stood in the boat to get a better view up ahead as Cassie and Matchstick edged the boat forward. The undergrowth was thick, trees and bushes over-hanging the river on both sides and touching in the middle. The wide river had narrowed to little more than a stream.

'The connection is hidden,' said Jay. 'Keep looking, it will be on the left-hand side, heading south.'

The boat nudged along the narrow gap between the branches of trees, Jay having to duck under from time to time. 'Stop rowing a minute,' she said, listening. 'You hear that?' she whispered.

'No,' came the reply from Cassie and Matchstick.

'Something,' said Ben.

Jay moved over to the side of the boat and strained her eyes to see into the bushes. 'Row back a bit,' she said.

Cassie and Matchstick dug in their oars, splashing water up and into the boat as they pushed against current to reverse. They dragged three deep strokes and then let the boat drift, coming to a halt and then relenting, to drift with the flow of the river again.

'There.' Jay's voice rose with excitement. Matchstick draped his oars over the foliage to stop them drifting. Jay pointed through the branches to a cave, a small opening into darkness, where the water from the River Wey diverged.

'That can't be it,' said Cassie. 'We won't even get the boat in there.'

'It's bigger than it looks, push back those bushes,' Jay pointed. 'This is it, pull us around, hurry.'

Jay's dad reached out and grabbed hold of a branch, helping Cassie and Matchstick manoeuvre the boat towards the entrance to the cave. Once they had pulled into the streamline of the cave, the boat obeyed their wishes and slipped into the pathway they needed, dipped over a shallow weir and into the cave.

'Heads down,' Matchstick shouted. The boat entered the cave and total darkness. Everyone ducked, unsure where the cave ceiling began as the boat picked up speed, bumping the sides of the cave as it shot through the channel. Jay held her breath, hoping jagged rocks wouldn't punch a hole in their boat and leave them upended in the water, unable to see.

'Jay!' her dad called, reaching out for her. 'Hold on to me.' Jay leaned into her dad and they huddled together, holding on to each other as well as to the seat.

Jay could just about make out that Matchstick was doing the same, holding tight and keeping down. 'Cassie,' Jay shouted, 'are you OK?'

Cassie shouted back that she was OK and the four of them could do nothing but keep down and hope.

After what seemed like forever, Jay felt the boat begin to slow. The noise abated a little and Jay sensed space, as if the cave had opened up above their heads. Light penetrated the darkness. The cave walls were nothing but black shapes, moving, distorting and fooling her. After another minute, the boat slipped down into a steep curve and out into a spectacular underground cavern, like a lost, subsurface lake.

The boat slowed almost to a stop. The four of them said nothing, all gazing at the spectacle that surrounded them. It was like being in the grand atrium of the London St Pancras Station but with trees and vines growing up the sides and to the roof. The roof itself was closed but for a series of gaps where light streamed through, illuminating the cavern. Water flowed from cracks in the rocks and dripped from the openings in the roof. All along the sides of the cave, birds nested among the tree roots. A fish broke the surface of the water and rolled over in the sunlight.

Jay's dad couldn't help his grin taking over his face as he looked at Jay, then back to where the fish slipped back beneath the surface. 'Rainbow trout,' he said.

'If only we had the spinners.'

Matchstick dipped his oars back into the water as the boat drifted, dragging them back on course for the point where the river continued downstream.

'Keep us moving, Matchstick,' said Jay. 'Sammy needs us.'

Cassie pulled hard on her oars, Matchstick following her lead.

'This place is unreal,' said Cassie as they left the tranquillity of the lake cavern and back into a tunnel, darkness enveloping them once more. Now the river widened and the roof was higher. The flow was slower and there was a little light leaking in from both ends. In the distance they could see daylight, and Jay knew that they were looking at the pool.

Jay's senses were electric. She could feel the power of the

earth surrounding them, the energy of the water beneath them. It was as if the vastness of the lake-cavern had followed them into the cave. The whispers came, stronger than before. She looked back over her shoulder towards the cavern. There was nothing but a bright, blinding light.

The round circle of turquoise light in the distance grew, and with it, the power and the intensity of the energy that flowed through Jay in waves. She felt Sammy, his waning life force, the infection flowing through his veins. He was hot, his pulse was weak, his breathing laboured. But he was fighting. And Stitch was there too, fighting with him.

'What's that?' said Cassie, as they passed an opening in the rock, at a joint where it looked like two rock masses had been displaced. Before they could register its significance, they had moved past, picking up speed as they drew nearer to the opening to the cave.

Jay felt the pressure of the Rother, building behind the blockage just feet from where Sammy and Stitch lay semi-conscious. It was about to blow, pushing rock and debris at bone-shattering force.

And she felt Marcus. Waiting. He was ready for them.

45

As the little rowing boat squeezed through the opening and into the pool, the pressure in Jay's head, the whispers, the energy, reached a crescendo.

The water from the unnamed river carried the four of them, in their boat, into the pool and followed with a thrust of water that flowed full-bore through the cave entrance, the light behind piercing the clear spray.

The flow from the river met a swelling from the depths of the pool The pool's surface rose, and together they shot into the air, up through the shaft and the chalk well, where they were met by a third stream of water and debris from the Rother. The jet from the Rother pushed through, taking Sammy and Stitch into the pool with Jay, her dad, Cassie and Matchstick.

Through the third and final connection, the Arun, the water bubbled and boiled, rising above the level of the main central cavern where Marcus and the other Readers stood, transfixed by the shaking beneath their feet, the deafening sound of the water shooting through from the connecting rivers. As Marcus turned towards the entrance to the cavern, the River Arun powered in and washed the three of them off their feet and out into the connecting caves.

In the pool, the Arun joined the Rother and the unnamed river to create a true convergence of the three rivers at the rising surface of the water in the pool. Inside, the swirl of energy and power from the earth, the water, the eco-systems, caught Jay and the others, suspending them in the eye of the storm.

* * *

THE EXPLOSION SUBSIDED, depositing Jay at the side of the pool. The water from each of the connections returned to their normal flows, the birds to their perches.

Jay's heart thumped and her fingers trembled. Ben pulled himself to stand next to Matchstick, over the other side of the pool. Stitch leaned down over the prone body of Sammy, his head bowed. No sign of Cassie. And no evidence of Marcus or the other Readers – though she could feel their presence.

She ran around the perimeter of the pool and joined Stitch. Sammy's eyes were closed. 'He's breathing,' said Stitch. 'I thought he was dead.' Jay held Sammy's head in her hand, cushioning it from the rocks. Stitch said, 'I really thought he was dead. When we were up there. I couldn't hear his breathing and couldn't feel any pulse.'

'Shh, Stitch,' said Jay. 'It's OK. We're going to get out of here.'

'I think I connected with him,' said Stitch.

'Really?'

Stitch nodded. 'I think so.'

Ben and Matchstick joined them, Ben leaning down to see Sammy. 'He OK?'

'Still out, but he's alive,' said Jay.

Her dad felt Sammy's head with the back of his hand and then leaned in to kiss his forehead. 'Bit of a temperature.'

'Where's Cassie?' said Stitch. Jay stood, looking around the pool. No sign of her. She called out but no response. She called out again, this time someone responding.

'Who's Cassie?' came the voice of Marcus as he emerged from the connection to the Arun, Jimmy and Drake close behind.

46

Stitch dragged Sammy back into an alcove in the side of the cliff to give him some protection from the bomb Jay sensed was about to go off.

Ben and Matchstick stood alongside Jay, facing Marcus and the other two Readers positioned the other side of the pool. 'They have more power than us,' said Ben.

'We have more to lose,' said Matchstick. Jay felt the power bubbling beneath her skin, the energy flowing up through the floor and into her body. She felt her own power connecting with that of her dad and Matchstick. She looked over at Marcus, standing tall. She felt his arrogance. As she studied him a time fracture passed over them, like a glitch. She could see that Marcus felt it too, and it shook his confidence.

Sammy still lay slumped in the corner, skin pale. 'Passed, has he?' Marcus said, and Jay sensed something lurking – a sadness, a vulnerability in Marcus's eyes. She looked again at her brother, then over to the Reader. Pieces slotted into place in her mind.

'You're his biological father,' Jay said, barely a whisper.

Marcus shook his head, as if trying to shake away Jay's words. 'We told you that this wasn't a game,' he said. 'Told you the easiest way for all of us was for you to come back with us.'

Jay looked at Ben and read the sadness in her dad. He'd known all along. He may not have admitted it to himself or anyone else, but Jay could see that he knew. 'He's my boy,' Ben said. 'In every way that matters, he's *my* boy.' Jay nodded and turned back to face the Readers.

'Here we are,' said Marcus. 'All together again.'

Jay felt Matchstick bristling with anger and determination. 'Wait,' said Jay, but Matchstick was already moving. He was in a trance, determination etched into his face. Jay and Ben followed, catching up with Matchstick as he stood less than three feet from Drake. Marcus and Jimmy a step behind, both smiling.

'That's better,' said Marcus.

Matchstick threw himself at Drake who put up his hands to hold him back. They connected, and sparks passed between them, their hands glowing as they wrestled and channelled their powers through their fingers. The sleeves of Drake's top caught fire and the two men stumbled to the floor, locked in a fiery battle.

Ben took the opportunity and lurched for Jimmy, taking him by surprise and knocking him to the floor, opting for a more traditional fist fight than Matchstick's use of powers. Jimmy was chunky and strong but no match for Ben's athleticism. He was younger and fitter, and with a series of punches, Jimmy landed on the floor with a thump.

Jay felt Marcus's power surround the man like a protective barrier. She took a step back, wavered, stepped forward again. He continued to exude arrogance.

He reached for her. She tried to lift her arms to protect

herself but they did not respond. He closed his hand around her neck and stepped closer, looking into her eyes and beyond. 'What level?' he said, to himself more than to Jay.

When Jay looked into Marcus she saw nothing. An abyss. His fear of the State was total; he would stop at nothing to destroy anyone he deemed a threat. Someone had something on him, some means to control him through fear. More than anything, his focus was that no one with power levels approaching that of his own survive. He tightened his grip on Jay's neck.

Matchstick pulled himself back to his feet by Jay's side, his hair still smoking from Drake having got the better of him. Her dad lay at her feet, knocked over by Jimmy who had reverted to his superior powers when Ben had gained the upper hand in their fist fight.

Marcus squeezed his hand tighter around Jay's neck.

Drake knocked Matchstick to the floor and knelt over him, his hand on Matchstick's forehead as if he were penetrating his mind.

Ben called out in pain as Jimmy focused in on him. He reached out for Jay but she was unable to break free of Marcus's grip.

Jay closed herself to the surrounding chaos. Her eyes shut tight. Then she opened to the whispers, the sounds and the power of her environment. The energy rose through her feet and the world stopped – ground to a crunching halt like a spanner had been lodged inside the cogs of the machine.

47

Marcus looked around the pool, wide-eyed, and Jay pulled herself from his grip. She stepped forward, shoving him back against the face of the cliff. She looked brave but coursed with fear. Would she would be able to prevent the Readers from taking them all away?

Marcus continued to gaze around the pool, mesmerised by the silence, the stillness, unconcerned by Jay having broken free of him. She focused in on him but he deflected her, brushing her off with his own power like she was nothing.

Jimmy and Drake began to stir, releasing themselves from the freeze, but Matchstick and Ben were still frozen in time.

As Drake and Jimmy stood, three further figures appeared at the cave entrance to the Arun. More Readers. Marcus turned and waved for them to join him. 'It's over, Jay,' said Marcus, now flanked by five powerful Readers. Jay knew that she could never overpower this many Readers, but she couldn't put the others at risk. Frozen, they were safe from danger.

Her time had run out, she'd not been able to connect completely, to harness the power well enough. Her legs trembled, she propped herself up on the chalk wall and looked around her, up into the sky.

Stitch's voice came through into Jay's head, calling her name. She turned to see that he remained frozen in time, leaning over the prone body of Sammy. As she looked at his statue, his scream came through once more. *Jay! Believe in yourself! You got this!*

She needed to be *surrounded* on all sides by the energy. In the water, or in the caverns. She needed to get the Readers into her own space, where the power would be with her. Without releasing time, Ben and Matchstick still frozen like rock, Jay turned to Marcus. 'What about the gateway?' she said. The Readers all looked at her and she put up the strongest shield that she could muster to prevent her thoughts leaking through.

'You know where it is?' Marcus said.

'If you let them go, I'll show you.'

'She doesn't know,' said Jimmy. 'She's lying.'

Marcus put up his hand to silence Jimmy, and Jay knew that he wouldn't be able to ignore the possibility. If he could locate the entrance to the gateway, and confirm that it existed, then he and the State would be able to take the ultimate control. They would contain the Given, cut off their entry to the source and diminish their power to worthless levels. The Readers may not be able to enter the depths of the Interland, for the energy of the source, but they could reduce it to all but dust.

'Show us,' Marcus said.

Jay walked through the middle of the group of Readers,

feeling their power aching for release. She led the way through to the main cavern, drawing the Readers away from the others, pausing just once to check that all six were following. The cavern smelled of bonfire, the remains of the notebooks and maps still smoking in the fire pit. She made her way towards the far wall of the cavern, the Readers filing in behind.

She turned to face Marcus as he stood at the front of the formation of Readers.

'Where is it?' said Marcus, looking towards each exit from the main cavern in turn.

Stitch's voice came to Jay again. Energy flowed through her, building her strength from the inside out. Whispers came. They guided her. Tingles travelled from the tips of her fingers through to her arms. This was the place. She could channel the power. Stitch was with her.

She had something that Marcus didn't have, the Readers didn't have. Their energy didn't come from nature as hers did.

She looked at Marcus as he cast his gaze around the room, still looking for the gateway. He was self-centred, too introspective to connect in any meaningful way with anyone else, or any other system. Jay was at one with the earth, the power of the water, and all living things that formed the walls, the floor, the ceiling.

'What is this,' Marcus said, stepping forward as Jay let her sleeve fall back into place. Jay felt the power pulsing through her body from below her feet. She no longer feared her power, she embraced it, welcomed it.

Marcus stepped closer. 'Whatever it is, it won't help you. I'm stronger. *We* are stronger.' He motioned towards the other Readers. 'You know there's nothing you can do about it. But you still have one option. Come in to *rehabilitation*.'

'Never.'

'Come with us. We could even save the boy, Sammy.' Jay saw through Marcus's words. He had no intention of allowing her and Sammy to return with him.

Her arms at her sides and fingers pointing to the floor, the power gathered strength. Her vision faded and Marcus whirled around in her head, his voice, his thoughts. She felt his hand close around her neck once more, and then the other hand. He squeezed. She closed her eyes, and the whispers intensified. He squeezed harder and air stopped passing into her lungs. He squeezed harder again, and pushed her up against the wall of the cavern, her feet leaving the floor.

Jay remained calm.

The five Readers were sucked towards the walls like magnets, the air forced from their lungs at impact. The walls of the cave behind Jay softened and shaped around her body, cradling her. The vines that penetrated the rocks twisted around her, supporting her weight, curling around Marcus's wrists. The water from the crevices in the rocks, the sun that penetrated through the shaft above their heads, poured down on them, covering them in clear, fresh water and powerful light.

Jimmy was the first to be pulled into the wall by the vines, screaming as his body amalgamated with the rock and then silent as he was crushed, his body now part of the undulating face of the cave wall. Drake and the others fought, but the vines remained strong, taking the Readers one by one into the stone.

Marcus pulled away, releasing Jay. 'What is this?'

'This is more than you, Marcus,' said Jay, her eyes sparkling with power, her feet barely touching the ground, her body tingling. She stepped towards him and he held his position. He reached out, not for her neck this time but to push her away. The force of his blow was re-directed back through his arm. 'Reciprocity,' said Jay through gritted teeth.

'Stop,' said Marcus, gathering himself once more.

'Every action has an equal but opposite reaction, Marcus. With every pain you inflict, there is a consequence. Reciprocity.' With this, Jay released the environment. The noise of the Arun pounded into the cavern. Marcus stiffened and used all of his power to try to penetrate Jay's mind. She felt it. Felt him digging at her defences. If he got in, he'd do damage this time, he aimed to destroy her. 'You're not strong enough, Marcus,' she said, re-directing his attack back on himself. With a rush of energy from all around her, Jay channelled her power to enter Marcus's mind, and she started to dig.

Marcus hit the floor just as the water from the River Arun crashed into the cavern, throwing both Jay and Marcus into a tornado of currents. As quickly as the water arrived, it drained back into the Arun and out through to the pool. Marcus dragged himself to his knees at Jay's feet, looking up into her eyes. Jay saw that his power had diminished. He had been reduced. He lifted a hand to the side of his face to feel the fresh scar, parallel to the old one, from temple to just below the chin. He shook his head in disbelief, stammering, 'No... n... no.'

PART VI

INTERLAND

48

Jay splashed through the water on the floor of the cavern towards the pool, the only sound the noise of the thundering river. She sensed the others, outside, her friends, her dad, and Sammy. As she reached the pool, she saw Cassie pulling herself from the water. She stood as Jay approached. 'Is it done?'

Jay nodded and Cassie wrapped her arms around her. 'What happened to you?' asked Jay.

'I don't know,' said Cassie. 'We shot through into the pool and then the world went crazy. I was up in the air, but under water at the same time. Where are the Readers?'

'Gone,' said Jay with confidence. 'Marcus is the only one left, but he's no threat. He has no power.'

'What about...?' said Cassie.

Sammy was lying on his back on the rocks, his dad crouching beside him.

'Is he OK? Is he hot?'

Her dad put his hand to Sammy's head. 'He's cold,' he said.

Jay pushed to get to Sammy. 'Is he breathing?' She

leaned down and put her ear to his mouth, then put a finger to his neck to feel for a pulse, her hands trembling.

His eyelids flickered and Jay breathed out with relief. She knew, sensed, that he was OK. She could feel him coming back to her. He had shaken off the infection and was growing in strength.

Cassie pushed past Jay, panic in her eyes. Sammy blew gently into her ear. She pulled away, rubbing her ear. 'What the...' Then she returned to listen again. This time, as she listened for his breathing, Sammy leaned forward and kissed Cassie on the side of her head. She drew away slowly this time, a grin forming as she sat up, not looking at Sammy, as Jay, Ben and Stitch laughed.

'You... Sammy,' said Cassie, still grinning. She kicked him lightly on the leg and he recoiled, wincing.

'Hey, not the ankle,' he said, pulling himself up to a sitting position. He dragged back his trouser leg to reveal much reduced swelling in his ankle. Cassie kicked him again, then leaned down and cuffed him on the back of the head before taking his face in her hands and landing a smacker of a kiss on his lips.

49

W ith their backs up against the chalk cliff, they gazed up through the opening in the trees to the clear sky above.

Jay had checked back in the main cavern but Marcus had gone, disappeared. It was possible he'd slipped into the pool and away through the exit when they'd been seeing to Sammy. Either that or he'd tried to head back upstream alongside the Arun. Whichever way he'd gone, Jay was sure he would be no threat to them. Even if he had anything left in him to fight with, there was nothing for him to come back to. No gateway that he'd ever be able to find.

Jay sat between Ben and Sammy, Matchstick on the other side of Ben. Sammy stretched out his leg and dipped his foot into the pool. Cassie stripped off her jeans and top and dived in, beckoning the others to join her. Sammy motioned towards his foot. Stitch shuffled up next to Sammy, leaving Cassie to it.

'How is it?' said Stitch.

'Better.'

'You had us worried.'

Sammy smiled at Stitch. 'Something of the healing hands you have there.'

Stitch shrugged. Jay smiled at her brother. 'We did it. Marcus is done.'

'*You* did it,' said Ben, leaning back and closing his eyes. 'I don't know what went on in that cavern between you and those Readers, but something big happened.'

'I realised something... from Sasha Colden.'

Matchstick leaned forward. 'Sasha Colden?'

Jay nodded. 'She had something to do with this place I think, she was more than just a level eight.'

'She's mythical. What they called *Connected*,' said Matchstick.

Ben huffed, 'I thought you didn't believe in this place?'

'She had a connection with the universe that no one else had.'

'What about Zadie Lawrence?' said Jay.

'She was strong. Tough woman. Level eight from what I heard, but not *Connected*.'

'So what's Jay then?' said Sammy.

'Connected,' said Matchstick, leaning back against the chalk cliff.

Cassie jumped out of the pool and Sammy threw her a top. She slipped her wet body back into her clothes and squeezed herself in between Sammy and Stitch. Jay looked up at the cliff face to see the falcon edging out onto its branch, as if to join them.

'Phoenix is back,' Sammy said.

Jay's dad looked up and grinned. 'Told you kids there was a phoenix down here. You should listen to your old dad.'

'Watch this,' Cassie said, jumping up and beckoning to the bird. With no further prompting, the falcon rocked off the branch and soared up into the sky, diving like it had before and pulling up in a graceful swoop to land this time on Cassie's outstretched arm.

Cassie let out a squeak of excitement and pain as it clenched onto her arm. Sammy stood, hobbled over to Cassie. He held out his arm, his hand touching Cassie's hand. The falcon edged along Cassie's arm like it was a tree branch and onto Sammy's arm. It remained still for a moment then turned to take in the others sitting on the floor, mouths half open, before launching into the air and back to its branch.

'Wow,' said Jay's dad. 'How'd' you do that, Sammy?'

'I have a thing for the birds, it seems,' said Sammy, hobbling back to sit down, with Cassie's help.

'What now?' said Cassie. 'If there's no gateway, what now?'

'Who said there's no gateway?' said Jay, matter-of-fact.

They all turned to look at her. Ben spoke. 'You know where it is? It's here?'

'Of course.' Jay smiled. 'It's here, I can feel it as clearly as I can feel gravity.'

'You can't *feel* gravity,' said Cassie.

'Where is it?' said Stitch, looking up and around himself.

'Me and Cassie passed the opening on the way in here, with Dad and Matchstick. On the unnamed river.'

'The cavern we passed through?' said Cassie.

'No,' said Jay, standing. 'Closer to here, there's a connection, an opening in the roof of the tunnel. I felt it more than saw it. Did you not feel the pressure change as we passed under it before emerging into here?'

Cassie shook her head, then Ben said, 'I felt something. But we can't get upstream, not against that flow. Are you sure there's something there?'

'There's something there for sure. Where it leads, I can only guess.' She walked towards the connection of the unnamed river as the others stood and brushed themselves down. 'As for working against the flow, that's less of a problem if you can *stop* the flow, freeze it for a little while.'

* * *

IT CAME EASIER THAN BEFORE. Jay had only to focus for a moment to stop the world on its axis before releasing her friends, her dad, and Sammy. As they joined in her static world, they each struggled in turn to take in this frozen, silent landscape. Jay ducked and stepped through the mouth of the cave, the opening to the unnamed river.

She led the way for a hundred metres upstream, the light fading with distance from the pool so that it was near pitch black by the time Jay stopped. She looked up to what looked like a darker section of the roof which could be an opening. 'Help me up,' she said to her dad. Matchstick and Ben formed a human frame for Jay to climb, with a steadying hand from Cassie. She managed to poke her head into the opening but could see nothing in the darkness. She jumped back down.

'We need more height.'

Stitch stepped forward as if he had a plan. 'If we can form a stronger base, with three of us, and we can get Cassie on the top, it might work. Cassie's the tallest and probably the lightest.'

With Ben and Matchstick at the base, and with Jay and Stitch creating a second level, they hauled Cassie up and onto Jay and Stitch's shoulders. She pushed herself up into the hole. 'I'm in,' she said.

'What's there?' said Matchstick.

There was no answer.

'Cassie?'

Jay moved beneath the hole to see Cassie's face lit with excitement as she pulled herself further into the hole.

Cassie turned and held a hand out for Jay to follow her up and then Stitch. Soon they were all inside except Ben.

'You'll have to jump,' said Jay. 'Jump with your hands outstretched and we'll get hold of you.' She called for Matchstick to help so that there were four of them leaning through the hole to catch Ben. On his second attempt, Matchstick and Cassie caught his hands, with Jay and Stitch grabbing on to help lift him through the hole.

'Thought I'd have to stay behind for a minute there,' said Ben as he pulled himself over the ledge and stood to join Jay.

'No chance,' said Jay. 'Not letting you go so easily this time.'

50

As Jay stepped into the connecting tunnel, her dad close behind, the other four stood facing a water- fall that poured from the roof and drained away below their feet into the cracks and crevices of the rocks.

'Through there?' said Stitch.

Jay nodded. 'That's it.'

Jay led the way through the waterfall and into a wider tunnel that opened out into a cavern. As she passed through the water, she saw three figures standing in the tunnel some twenty metres ahead.

Jay immediately recognised Reuben, but not the other two – a woman in her forties, and an older man. Cassie came through the waterfall and then broke into a run. 'Grandad!' she called, launching herself at the man and throwing her arms around him. He rocked backwards and laughed, embracing his grandaughter. She pulled away then, and pushed out at him, scolding him.

'I'm sorry, Cassie. It was the only way.' Cassie hugged him again, holding on tight. As Cassie withdrew from his embrace, her grandad nodded towards Reuben. Cassie stared. When it clicked, she stepped back a pace.

'Cassie,' he said. 'Now you're here, I can explain. *We* can explain.' Cassie looked unsteady on her feet and Sammy stepped forward to hold on to her arm.

'You must be Reuben,' Sammy said.

Reuben nodded. 'Old friend of Cassie's. I came down here to train as a Runner. I couldn't say anything, Cassie. I'm sorry.' He stepped towards her but Cassie retreated.

'We can explain everything,' the woman said.

'Who are you?' Stitch asked the woman.

Jay spoke. 'Zadie Lawrence.'

Zadie smiled at Jay. 'I've waited a long time to meet you, Jay. It's a pleasure. And we will be forever grateful for what you did down there. Marcus was the biggest threat to the sanctuary of our world.'

'He might still be down there,' said Stitch.

Jay and Zadie both shook their heads and spoke at the same time. 'His power has gone.'

Zadie indicated for Jay to follow them into the caves.

'Where are we going?' asked Jay.

'To the place you've been looking for. You've found it. This is where you can rebuild your strength, amongst friends. The community here has been waiting for this day, waiting for a reason to believe that we can make a change. We have some work to do, but this is the beginning of a process to take back our world.'

Ben stepped forward. 'Look, Zadie, we came here to escape from the fighting, the Readers. We didn't come to join an army, if we wanted a war we'd have...'

'Dad, it's OK,' Sammy said. 'How many people are down here?'

'Nearly a hundred,' said Zadie. 'About half with powers.'

'How many level eights?' asked Stitch.

'There is only one,' said Reuben, looking at Zadie.

The five from above ground fell into step, following the others into a new world.

51

Jay looked back as they walked through a warren of tunnels, not convinced she'd be able to find her way back to the entrance if she needed to. As they approached a large opening, the sound of talking, laughter and the chinking of crockery leaked with the light into the tunnel ahead.

Cassie looked deflated, as if they'd failed when she should be elated that they'd won, they'd found what they were looking for. As they followed Zadie into the great cavern, Stitch propped Sammy up with an arm around his waist.

The bustle of activity faded and all faces turned to observe the new arrivals. Jay reckoned on there being about fifty or sixty people in the room, and still it looked big. Light filtered down from the roof where Jay guessed there must have been an opening into the trees, much like at the outside pool. The smell of food made Jay's mouth water and she realised she'd not eaten properly for days. In the middle of the room, three large pots of stew bubbled away, the smoke and fumes rising through a chimney-like construction and into the roof. She scanned the faces, old and young, some with smiles and others with curiosity but all with a semblance of hope, as if in expectation of something from their visitors.

Zadie Lawrence called for attention. The room quieted. She introduced Jay and the others as *new members* and the room gave a smattering of applause. 'Please make them welcome, we have some special abilities with our new members, powers that we hope will help us to re-invigorate our community and bring back some of the magic that left us when Sasha passed.'

As Zadie stepped down, a young boy of no more than twelve or thirteen handed her two bowls of steaming stew. She passed a bowl to Jay and motioned for her to sit. More children came, handing bowls of food to Sammy and the others, each of them finding seats where they were accompanied by others introducing themselves. Sammy sat with Jay and Zadie.

'Who's that?' Jay nodded at a photograph on the wall behind where they sat.

'I'd have thought you would know?' said Zadie.

'Sasha Colden,' said Jay, now recognising the face of the woman whose autobiography she had in her backpack. She was older in the photograph than in her picture in the book. Her features were more distinct, the lines and creases in her face hinting at her great knowledge and power.

'She founded this community. She is the Godmother of the Given.' Zadie looked at the picture with affection and, Jay sensed, sorrow, and even a little guilt. 'She passed before I joined. Despite the Runners' attempts to bring me in to work with her, I resisted. I thought I knew how to stand up to the State, and their attempts to wipe us off the face of the earth. Direct action. Of course the authorities knew better.

They had their own weapons. People like Marcus, who you dealt with out there. It was Marcus's superior who reduced me after the protest.' She pointed to the scar down the side of her face, much like the one Marcus had, and like the second scar that Jay had given Marcus when she reduced him. 'I never thought I'd recover from this.'

'His superior?' said Jay. She had assumed that Marcus was at the top of the food chain of the Readers. The thought of him having a superior sent shivers up her spine. Zadie nodded. 'How did you get away, to get here?' Jay asked.

Zadie looked towards Reuben, who was deep in conversation with Stitch. 'He brought me in. I was his first apparently. He'd only recently become a Runner. Saved my life. My power had been drained when he found me. It took me a good few weeks to recover down here. It was almost like learning my powers from the start. It came back eventually.' She turned her head to the side to show Jay the scar. It had a silvery sheen like Marcus's, and ran from her temple to under her chin, just like his. 'Battle scar,' Zadie said.

'I've seen one like that. On Marcus.'

'I heard,' said Zadie. 'He was made a Reader in the early days. We don't know if it was voluntary or by force. Someone went to work on him and by the time he came out the other side he was a fully signed up agent of the State.'

Jay exchanged a look with Sammy, who gave a slight shrug. 'When did Sasha die?' he asked Zadie.

Zadie turned to him. 'A few years before Reuben brought me in.' Zadie explained that Sasha Colden spent years alone in the underground at first. She had been drawn to the place and abandoned her normal life to re-imagine herself. She became a recluse. 'Story says that she was forced to leave her family and her son.' She looked at Ben.

Ben's mother had died before Jay had been born. Jay had

never known her grandmother. Old Alf Harvey had talked about her, but... She turned back to Zadie as she continued. 'She spent years without seeing or speaking to another human. The world assumed she'd died. Then Pete and Jack found her.' She nodded towards Cassie's grandad. 'They found the pool at the gateway to the Interland when they were kids, and they were still visiting the place when Sasha connected with them. Cassie's grandad is older than Sasha would be if she were still alive.' Zadie smiled. 'It was Pete and Jack who helped her find her purpose again.'

Ben came over, moving closer to the portrait on the wall, studying Sasha Colden's picture.

'What happened then?' asked Sammy.

'Sasha reached out and brought in a small group with high-level powers. We think at levels six and seven. She established some protocols to protect what she'd built. They made the level sevens Runners, people who would leave the underground just once a year to bring in others who were at risk. But *only* once a year, to ensure the security of the Interland.'

'Any other level eights?' asked Jay.

'No,' Zadie said, and went on to explain how the community continued to grow around Sasha Colden, with Jack and Pete remaining the custodians of the pool, the link between the outside and the underground. 'Before Sasha died, she said to those that were here that there would be another like her. Another level eight.'

'That was you?' said Sammy.

'No,' Zadie replied. 'I am a level eight for sure.' She showed her wrist, the crisp and distinct figure eight undeniable. 'But Sasha meant more than just a level eight. We think she was referring to someone who would be *connected*, like her. The connected power comes only through genes, through blood relations.' Zadie looked at Jay, who averted her gaze. Zadie turned to Sammy. 'Do you have a level, Sammy?'

Sammy shook his head, pulling back his sleeve to show that there was nothing there, not even a smudge.

'I sense you have something. How old are you?'

'Sixteen,' said Sammy.

'Then you have a little while to go.'

Zadie looked up as a boy around Jay's age came over to relay a message. 'All three Runners are back in, Zadie.'

'Thank you, David. Can you let them know that we will need to get all the Runners together later, including Reuben?' The boy nodded and turned on his heels.

'How many Runners are there?' asked Sammy.

'Just four, including Reuben. There are only four in here at level seven. How about you, Jay? Anything on your wrist yet?' asked Zadie.

Jay pulled back her own sleeve, the figure eight clear. Zadie reached out for Jay's hand, pulling her closer so that she could inspect her wrist. 'Definitely an eight. Question is whether there's anything else coming.'

'You mean a "C"?' said Jay.

Zadie nodded. 'There's something I need to show you when you're ready, after you've rested.'

52

'We held a *funeral*,' Cassie shouted at her grandad, drawing looks from around the room. 'I cried for you, for weeks.'

A young girl brought them some food and Jack motioned for Cassie to sit. He explained the circumstances of his entry to the pool, and how he and his childhood friend, Pete, had looked after the entrance caverns for so many years. He was Sasha Colden's closest confidant. He had a duty to the Given. He pulled back his sleeve to reveal a number four.

'You...' Cassie stuttered, 'you have power. You never told me.'

'I was an unusual case. My mark was never clear. Even into my sixties, there was nothing but a smudge. After I brought Reuben in...'

'*You* brought Reuben in?'

He looked down at his bowl of stew, lifting a spoon to his lips. He took a deep breath. 'Reuben has something special, something different. Like your friend, Jay, but with a different calling. He was born to be a Runner. Sasha Colden had her eye on him from when he was just a boy, and my job was to keep him safe until the time was right for him to come in. When he turned eighteen and his mark started to appear, I had to bring him in. He wouldn't have lasted a month outside.'

'No one said anything to me. No message. Nothing.'

'It was forbidden. And for good reason. If just one of those things, those Readers, found their way to the gateway then all this would be at risk.' He looked around the cavern. 'And without this, the Given would be hunted to extinction.'

Cassie finished her food. Her body felt heavy, as if saturated, no longer able to support itself. Her grandad put a hand on her arm and she looked him in the eye. She smiled at him, the beginning of an uneasy forgiveness.

Sammy had been taken away for medical treatment. Matchstick and Ben were talking to a group over by the cooking pots. Jay was with Zadie Lawrence. As she took in her surroundings, Cassie's gaze settled on Stitch and Reuben, talking together, Stitch being introduced to two men who seemed very excited to meet him. Reuben looked over and caught Cassie's eye. He excused himself from Stitch and made his way over to Cassie and her grandad. Cassie looked away.

'Hey,' said Reuben.

Cassie's grandad stood, shaking Reuben's hand. 'You've done well today I hear?'

'It's been a good week, what with these new arrivals, and some positive movement with the level seven I saw today. Our strength is growing.'

'What level seven?' said Cassie.

Reuben smiled. 'One we've been tracking for some time. He's from the north. Just turned eighteen, little older than you, Cassie.'

'You track all of them?'

'Not all. The ones we know about. Little by little. The more we bring in, the more Runners we can train and the more we can track. We need level sevens to become Runners.'

'Why?'

'Because it's only level sevens and higher that can resist the Readers. We can, with training, prevent the divulgence of information. Readers can't get in our heads, as long as we know how to block.'

'So no one else leaves?' Cassie said, an indignant tone in her voice.

Her grandad spoke. 'No. That's why we have to be sure, we have to wait for people to choose their own path, come when they are ready.'

Cassie's head reeled. The thought of being trapped in this place, the supposed sanctuary turned prison. A tomb. 'You can't stop people leaving!'

'Cassie.' Reuben put a patronising hand on her arm and she pulled it away. 'The point is, the *plan* is, that we all leave, once we are ready, and the time is right for us to make the changes for the better above ground. We hope you and your friends will be part of that.'

Cassie put her head in her hands, still unable to accept the situation as her fate, as the only option. For something purporting to be freedom, she felt trapped.

'Let me show you around,' Reuben said, holding out a hand to help Cassie up. Her grandad sat back down, nodding at Cassie to go with Reuben.

She ignored his hand but stood. 'OK,' she sighed. 'Let's have a look around this dungeon.' She looked over at Jay, laughing with Zadie Lawrence. 'Where's Sammy?' she said.

'Receiving treatment, I'll show you.'

Reuben led the way from the main cavern into one of the connecting tunnels. The sounds of voices faded. They walked in silence for a while, passing several other tunnel connections that branched off from the main pathway. After a minute or so, having walked maybe a hundred yards, they entered another, smaller cavern, a kind of lobby to an adjacent room that was different to the other rooms. This one looked as though it had been constructed by hand, rather than naturally formed. It had vertical walls and an arched roof, mined so that records could be efficiently stored from floor to ceiling in spaces protected from water that might penetrate through cracks and holes, yet illuminated by the light from the light-well above. There were some six or seven people in the room, all working at their own makeshift desks, poring over the records and notes.

'This is where we store records,' said Reuben. 'Intelligence from the Runners, and from other sources we have on the outside that pass information to the Runners when we go out.'

'What's it for?' said Cassie, turning to see a man working in the room approach.

The man smiled the broadest of grins. 'Cassie?' he said. It was old Alf Harvey, the bookseller. Before Cassie could argue, Alf embraced her, a tear edging from the corner of his eye. 'Is Jay here?'

Cassie nodded, Alf drew her in to another hug and then turned to leave. Reuben smiled. 'He's been looking forward to you guys coming in.'

'Jay thought he'd been taken,' said Cassie.

Reuben continued his tour. 'Intelligence on the Given. Our aim is twofold: one, to contact people who need an escape from persecution; and two, to predict where the powers will be, with whom they are concentrated, so we can get to them before the authorities do, offer them an alternative to incarceration.' Cassie thought again how the difference between incarceration above ground and entrapment underground might not be so great. 'There's a whole world of difference, Cassie. Like you wouldn't believe.'

Cassie pulled back her sleeve again to take another look at her smudge. Reuben took a step towards her. 'I didn't know...'

'You wouldn't know, you weren't there,' Cassie said, then felt stupid for sounding so bitter. *Childish*, she thought to herself.

'It's OK,' said Reuben.

'Will you *please* stop reading me without asking,' Cassie shouted at Reuben so that he stepped back from her. 'Just because you can read me, doesn't mean you have permission. Is that what you lot do in here? Read whatever you like, don't bother asking?'

'Sorry.'

'Just don't.' Cassie turned away from him.

'Your friend Stitch has a level too.'

Cassie turned. 'Stitch? What level?'

'It's not clear yet, it's a strange one. He showed me his wrist, and it doesn't look like a number. I've never seen anything like it and I've seen a lot of people's markings.'

'What is it then?'

'It looks like the beginnings of the letter "C". Like Sasha Colden, but without the number, just the letter. In Sasha, we thought that the "C" depicted her *connection* with all things. But with Stitch, I don't know. He's gone to see Zadie.'

Cassie thought about Stitch, how he seemed to be so connected with Jay. He knew better than anyone what she was thinking, what she needed. He was the one who heard her call for help the night the Readers came.

'You have a level then?' said Reuben.

Cassie shrugged. 'Nothing distinct. But there's something coming.'

'Can I see?'

Cassie turned back to Reuben and lifted her sleeve. He took her hand in his and she could feel his presence, his energy. She tried to remain calm. She had loved this boy for as long as she could remember. But she'd got over him. He disappeared, and she had moved on. She was not about to allow him back inside her head.

'Probably a level one or something so nothing to get excited about,' she said.

Reuben stepped closer to Cassie, leaning towards her so she could feel his warmth. 'Now even a level one is...'

'Thought you were showing me around?' Cassie interrupted, pulling away and turning back to the entrance. Reuben followed her out of the records room and led her away to another set of tunnels and another cave.

'Sammy!' Cassie called, seeing him prone on a bed with someone leaned over examining his ankle. He had his hands behind his head. He turned to Cassie with a grin.

'How is it?' she asked.

The man tending to Sammy's ankle mumbled, 'Nasty. Not broken but possibly a cracked bone and certainly a deep gash. It looks like it's had some attention but Sammy's memory is shot, do you know who treated it?'

'No one,' said Cassie. 'Strangely enough there aren't many doctors down there.'

'He'll have to keep off it for a while, we don't have the means for a plaster cast down here right now but I'll strap it up.' He looked up and smiled at Cassie. 'I'm Tommy.'

Sammy retained his grin. 'Hear that? Smashed it. Been on it for hours, days, and it's smashed to pieces. Scale of one to ten on the pain: eleven. Scale of one to ten on the courage and bravery: eleven. Isn't that right, Tommy?'

Tommy smiled as he kept his concentration on the strapping he was applying to Sammy's ankle. 'Right, Sammy. Brave warrior.'

Reuben laughed. 'Good to see your spirits are up, Sammy,' he said. 'I'll show you the rest of the network, Cassie? The residential area is through the back there...'

'I think I'll stay here with Sammy for a bit.'

Reuben nodded and turned to leave. 'Another time,' he said. 'We've got time. It's good to see you again, Cassie.'

Cassie turned her attention back to Sammy, taking a seat next to his bed and reaching for his hand.

53

J ay noticed that the air was cooler at the lower levels, and the walls were damp with a constant trickle from above. The only light came from a candle Zadie held before them as they walked.

'Mind your step,' Zadie said over her shoulder.

After their welcome meal, and having had some time to rest and store her things in the residential section of the underground, Zadie had come to find Jay. They talked on their way down to the lower levels. Zadie said that Stitch had come to see her, displaying signs of a mark that no one had seen before.

'I've heard of such a marking,' Zadie said to Jay.

'Someone else down here?' asked Jay.

'No. Just rumours. The only verified marking with a "C" is Sasha Colden's, but hers with the number eight as you know. But I heard rumours of another with a "C" and no number. Someone connected closely to Sasha Colden. Someone with whom Sasha had a special connection. A direct connection.'

They reached the bottom of the rock steps and Jay

watched as Zadie walked the perimeter of the room, lighting a series of candles set into alcoves in the walls. The room revealed itself with a central pillar where water trickled down from above and disappeared into the ground.

'Look here,' said Zadie.

Jay peered around the pillar at where Zadie was motioning. Three separate streams of water trickled in at a rate no greater than that from a tap, each a different hue. They combined at the centre of the pillar and disappeared in a single flow into an opening in the rock below. Jay recognised it as like a mini version of the confluence of the rivers above ground.

'This is the Rother.' Zadie pointed to the gentlest trickle of water. 'This is the Arun, and this one is the unnamed river.'

Jay could see the sparkle in the emerald-green of the unnamed river water. At their convergence, the water bubbled and boiled, pushing back up in a geyser-like spray before discharging through a hole in the rock and away through the floor.

'Who built this?' said Jay, mesmerised by its beauty, its intricate functionality.

'No one. It's natural. I am told that it's been here from long before any of us arrived, even before Sasha Colden was here.'

'What does it mean?' Jay asked, unable to take her eyes off the continually changing shapes created by the water which, in turn, cast shadows across the walls from the candles around the perimeter.

'This is what we hoped you might be able to help us with. We don't know for sure because there's no one here that was around when Sasha Colden was here. Only Jack,

Cassie's grandad, but he was never inside the hill, in the underground.'

'How should I know?' asked Jay, a half-hearted question given that deep inside she sensed there was something connecting her with this place, this room, and with Sasha Colden.

'Show me your wrist again,' said Zadie, stepping towards Jay and drawing back her sleeve. Jay tore her eyes away from the confluence and looked down at her wrist. The number eight had sharpened, its edges defined and black as night against her pale arm. With it, the letter "C" had started to form. It remained blurry at its edges but distinguishable as a letter "C".

'Eight-C,' said Zadie. 'Like we thought.'

'I can feel something,' said Jay, her eyes returning to the confluence, the joining of the three streams of water at six levels below the pool at the surface. An energy rose in her chest, a pulsating vibration beneath her feet. Zadie spoke but her words became lost in the whispers that came from all sides – from the walls, the floor, and from the streams of water flowing through the pillar before her. The whispers grew louder, clearer. The message was more transparent than before, translated to a language that had become like Jay's native tongue. She absorbed the energy, the knowledge, the needs and the desperation of her surroundings. She understood. And, they understood.

JAY WOKE on the floor of the cave, Zadie and Stitch both in her face, calling her name.

'What? Is that you, Stitch?'

Zadie and Stitch helped Jay to a sitting position. 'She's OK,' said Stitch.

'How did you know?' Zadie said to Stitch.

'I heard her calling, inside. I just knew.'

Jay groaned, 'Look at your wrist, Stitch.'

Stitch turned his hand to show his wrist. No number but a crystal-clear letter "C". He put his wrist up alongside Jay's, where her "8C" had also crystallised in contrast.

'You're Jay's connection,' said Zadie. 'Sasha Colden had one too. Someone who connected and completed the power, the connection with the environment. Everything.'

Stitch smiled. 'I always knew I'd be the chosen one.'

Jay laughed, pulling herself up to stand. 'So what does this mean?'

Zadie smiled, taking Jay's arm on one side, Stitch taking the other. 'It means that you two are the next generation of power. You will help us finish what Sasha Colden started.'

'And what was that?' said Stitch.

'Taking back what belongs to us, and to everyone else. Re-connecting the people, and the environment.'

Jay felt strength returning to her body as she climbed the steps, the force of energy that was the Interland supporting her from the inside, and the arm of Zadie and the shoulder of Stitch helping her up from the outside.

Jay and Stitch entered the central cavern. Ben sat on a rock with a notebook. He stood and opened out an arm to pull Jay into a side-by-side hug.

'What's the notebook?' said Jay.

Her dad nodded towards the portrait of Sasha Colden. 'One of Mum's diaries, it seems,' he smiled. 'Your grand-mother's notes.'

'Thought so,' Jay said. She pulled back her sleeve to show her dad the "8-C" on her wrist.

* * *

CASSIE ENTERED the cavern with Sammy, propping him up on his strapped-up leg as they shuffled over to join them. Jay's dad helped Cassie get Sammy sat down on a rock. 'How is it?'

Sammy smiled. 'It's good, Dad, I'm on the mend.'

Cassie nudged Jay and turned her arm to show the inside of her wrist. The beginnings of a number seven were clearly visible. Jay had known that Cassie had power growing, but a level seven surprised all of them, most of all Cassie.

Jay took a breath, looked up into the vast ceiling of the cavern, shards of light penetrating from the sky above. Energy pulsed through her body and she relaxed into it. For the first time, she allowed her power to flow without fear of detection.

At last, she was free. Her new environment, the Interland, was a place to savour and to protect. It was a place that would provide a foundation, and spark the beginning of a new journey – one that would take the fight back to the world above.

End of Book #1

THANK YOU!

I hope you enjoyed my first book in the Interland series.

Reviews are really important for new authors like me. If you can spare a minute to leave a short review on your preferred store, just a sentence or two, then I'd be very grateful - Thanks!

Link to leave a review (if you're reading the eBook...!)

If you've not joined my Reader Club, where you can keep up to date on forthcoming publications, news and freebies to go with the INTERLAND series - including a free eBook prequel called *The Reader*, an insight to Marcus and his background - then please join by visiting my website -

www.garyclarkauthor.co.uk

ABOUT THE AUTHOR

Gary graduated from the University of Surrey in the UK with a degree in Engineering, embarking on a career that has taken him all over the world from the Far East to the Americas. He is a graduate of the Faber Academy and Curtis Brown creative writing programmes. Now a father of three, he has settled with his family close to where he grew up on the edge of the South Downs in Sussex, where he indulges his love of books, and passion for writing.

I'd love to hear from you so feel free to contact me on the email address below - let me know what you thought of the book. And look out for the sequel - *Interland*.

gary@garyclarkauthor.co.uk

Or visit my website

www.garyclarkauthor.co.uk

ACKNOWLEDGMENTS

Thanks to my family for enduring the months of my squirrelling myself away to write, my distraction with my characters and their plight, and my endless questions about what they would do in Jay's situation. Ella, Evan, Ash - you have always been my greatest advocates - you are my inspiration. And, Dr Jude, you are the best.

Thanks to my early readers - especially Andrea, Dave, Hannah, and Mum (of course x).

Thanks also to my wonderful *'slack'* writing group who have provided insightful feedback along the way and helped me to keep going - especially Celia, Andrew, Laura, Kirsty, Kate, Julie, and James.

First published 2021 GCL Books.

www.garyclarkauthor.co.uk

Paperback ISBN 978 1 8384010 0 9

Printed in Great Britain
by Amazon